Unt

Jack Grisham

Punk ★ Hostage ★ Press

Untamed

Jack Grisham

ISBN 978-0-9851293-8-5

© Punk Hostage Press 2013

Punk Hostage Press

P.O. Box 1869

Hollywood CA, 90078

www.punkhostagepress.com

Editor:

Iris Berry

Associate Editors:

Dyanne Gilliam

Michelle Lewis

Introduction

A. Razor

Cover Design and Illustrations:

Scott Aicher

Editors Acknowledgments

There are many people Jack would like to thank, who without their love, support, friendship and generous contributions, this book would not be possible. In Jack's own words—"my hat is tipped."

Lois Darleen, Julia Kwong, Iris Berry, A. Razor, Kyle, Mark Hammer, Kevin Foster, Vern Gervais, Joe Porter, Connie, John Bishop, Kathy Shanley, Chris Turner, Kathy Guthrie, Jeff Claire, Catherine Pilchowski, Anna Kwong, Blaze J Hurley, Darrin Weedon, Charlie McDonald, Chele Rubendall, Josh Godar, Mel Schantz, Maggie Ehrig, Paul Roessler, Tami R Stover, Tom Callinan, Kristen Core, Erik Frank Urquidi, Johnny Wedell, Ron Grotjan, Scott A. McSeveney, Lila Sadeghi, Thomas Jones, James Stewart, William D. Gould, Kelly Henry, Andrew Rohan, Garrett Biggs, Mick Haven, Bob 'Buzz' Harris, T.S.O.L., and many others...

There are many people Punk Hostage Press would like to thank who have been extremely supportive in the making of this book.

Beyond Baroque for their care and support. Richard Modiano and Carlye Archibeque who have both been truly wonderful and supportive, as always.

Scott Aicher for his incredible cover art and illustrations. For always being available and willing to help in every way possible.

Lee McGrevin for all of our technical needs and for his endless loyalty and care. Sonny Gordiano for his constant devotion and all his hard work and willingness when he is needed most.

Dave Brinks for his love, patience, support and inspired enthusiasm for Punk Hostage Press and *Untamed*.

Special thanks to Pleasant Gehman, Bob Forrest, Jerry Stahl, Wyatt Doyle, John Albert, Anele D. and A. Razor for all his hard work, vision and dedication.

A very special thank you to everyone who supports Jack Grisham in all that he does. We couldn't do this without you.

Last, but certainly not least, we would like to thank Jack Grisham for his generosity of spirit and all that he does for many communities.

Iris Berry   2013

Introduction

Life has a way of facing us down when we least expect it. Moments that become overtaken in milliseconds by shifting winds, instincts, impulses or subconscious desires that can blindside us without warning. The measure of life can be the way we ride these changes, weather these storms and extricate ourselves from the wreckage. As we do this, we will notice, not everyone makes it through intact, or makes it through at all, for that matter. The debris piles up in the soul, the scars last forever. This is a collection of stories that plunge the senses deep into the tactile memories of those moments and give the undiluted vision of the wilderness inside the last acts of desperate hearts and pathological minds.

There is a touching grace that is woven in between the chaos and order of the story as it unravels in each vignette. Sometimes it is only a slender thread that traipses off into the pathos, but it is there throughout in the voice of the humanity as it is besmirched, battered and bruised, but never is driven into a complete submission.

Jack Grisham spins these tales from the heart, even from the point where it has been bruised or torn asunder, straight out into the universe as a primal cry of a wild beast let loose on wanton rampage. The words are compacted into dangerous bludgeons in one voice, then lilts into sorrowful songs of stoic suffering in another. The poignant melodrama that unfolds in each story is crafted as artistically as stone arch on a rocky point that juts out into the stormiest of seas. All the while it wears the cool skin of a survivalist creature that defies any cliché pantomime of trite language or colorless imagery. This skin is worn as wild adornment in rugged demeanor as it struts into dangerous territory where instincts rule the animalistic urges and self-control is a bargain that begs to get struck.

This collection of streetwise encounters is an esoteric submergence in a world gone mad, taken to its limits, then taken a bit further down the road for a ride that will send some chills up the spine of the most jaded cynic, yet give relief to the most beaten down souls in search of redemption. Jack Grisham creates a perspective that can easily be identified with, but seldom gets the opportunity to have a voice of its own, especially so clear and distinct a voice as it is given here, in line after line, all throughout every narrative, from every angle.

The stories in this collection come punctuated with the edgily artful illustrations of Scott Aicher. Each piece gives dimension and representation to the story and helps to make the book into a moving visual experience that conquers the senses by setting them free to envision this world that is outlined in the story, but accentuated in the artwork as well. The result is a tandem realization of the wordsmith and the graphic design into a singular vein of trajectory that helps launch the mind of the reader full tilt into the cosmos and back. Scott Aicher has definitively captured the essence of the writer's intentions and has connected them in a way that makes for some vivid projections that illuminate what even the blind dog can't see.

Jack has been an inspiring individual as a self-styled musical bard that set a standard for highly energized personal freedom since the early days of the So-Cal punk rock music juggernaut of the late 70's. He has maintained an integrity for his presentation as being the most ferocious he can muster in the face of the abject mediocrity of the status quo pop culture mausoleum that people tend to create in and for in these modern days way past the decline. In this book he resurrects his ferocity as a writer and storyteller that is turning the belly of the beast inside out in order to expose the guts of the whole thing for the world to see. Don't look away for a second, he has yet to be tamed.

A. Razor   2013

"You've lied to me, cheated on me,
used me and tried to kill me on numerous occasions,
and yet, I just keep on loving you. Maybe one day, when you've
matured, you'll look in the mirror and say, "thank you."
But until then Mr. Jack, let's just agree to disagree
and try to get along."

A thank you to my loves…

Anastasia, Georgia, and Robin…

I Love a Parade

Main Street was a traveling zoo on July 4th, with great helium animals marching past the windows of his apartment near the corner. He resided on the third floor, which gave him a perfect angle to view the beasts of the parade as they passed by. Today was his favorite day of the year. The crowds outside, had swelled so that he was almost able to feel their touch—their mirth and Independence Day spirit climbing toward his heart—almost. When was the last time someone had come upstairs and knocked on his door? The manager of the building had been up two months ago, but he wasn't sure if that really counted—although, hand delivering a "raise of rent" notice was a very nice gesture. The phone hadn't rung either. The last call was from his ex-wife's new "friend" telling him that if he didn't stop harassing her, a restraining order would be issued. He hadn't harassed her; he just wanted to get things straight, and the fact that she hadn't called him herself had given him some hope that maybe she still cared enough to not want to hurt him—of course, that hope was gone now. She was no better than last year's streamers, colorful paper ropes, so promising and so beautiful, only to be swept into the street and dispatched to the trash. He looked out the window as a large Sponge Bob merrily floated by. He liked that cartoon show, although he was surprised that Bob was floating down the street in an orderly fashion; the character was, after all, a bit unruly. The thought made him smile.

He grabbed the rope he'd recently purchased and had laid neatly coiled on the dining room table. It was a strong, light piece of cut mountain climbing cord—a touch expensive, but it was worth it, if it didn't break. He got down on his knees and wrapped one end of the rope around a solid oak leg of the table, and then he tied it off. It left him a length of about thirty-two feet, or the distance across a living room and two stories down, if you were tossing it out a window.

He walked into his bedroom where the pictures from last year's vacation were still lying on the floor where he'd placed them. He'd laid the photos out as a sort of visual timeline, a picture map of a trip to Big Sur that he'd taken with his ex-wife. He'd been imagining that if he could somehow walk down that path he could go back, bring her home, and somehow re-live their time together—it hadn't worked. The plan had seemed like it could've been successful, or at least kind of successful, after he'd had a few drinks, but in the morning it made less sense.

He remembered thinking that if he'd kept pictures since childhood—from his first day in the world—that maybe he *could* have removed a shot or two and led an entirely different life. What were they using to take pictures back then, Polaroids? *Huh.* Even in 1970 they were beginning to lose touch with slow, meaningful, relationships. Everybody wanted fast—instant gratification—nobody wanted to work on anything anymore, really try before you cast something, or someone, aside. Even the parade had gotten quicker. Each year the long, winding, hang-on-to-the-tail-in-front chain had skipped by faster and more hurried. It was sad. He paused in thought.

There was a band going by in the street below. He listened as the sound came close, hung for a verse or two, and then moved on down the street before the chorus. He wondered if the blow-up Sponge Bob enjoyed this tune.

He carefully began to remove his clothes and looked at himself in the mirror. He wasn't a bad looking man. He was tall, what some might consider handsome, and he still had a full head of thick brown hair, but inside he was through. If someone would have poked him, that is, if they had gotten close enough, his hard outer shell would have easily broken and the thick, black gelatinous muck of defeat would have leaked from inside. Shit, he hadn't thought of that. He hoped he fell clean, without a cut, because he'd hate to ruin the parade by raining muck on the spectators.

How'd it go bad anyway, his marriage to Katherine? He'd been kind and gracious, or so he thought, loved her more than anyone ever could. But she did say he was angry, not at her—well, maybe once or twice at her—but at everything. He didn't think it was true. Sure, he had the complaints of any man; *why the fuck do some get this and I get that? What have I done to deserve the short end of the stick? How come I can never find a fucking parking space when I need one?* But was he angry? No, just tired of being pushed around, and he had a healthy willingness not to be bullied or used by anyone.

He thought back to the day she'd left. He'd come home late as usual, and he was tired, but not overly so. He walked in, the same as he did every night, but this time he walked into nothing. It was empty, missing, gone. She just wasn't there. There was no note, no explanation, and no mess. She didn't even really take anything, just some clothes and a photo of the two of them in Big Sur. But, it was as if the house had just… died. Yes, it was just the skin of a place that used to be lived in and, without realizing it, the picture of them together held all the power. It was the heart of his home. A simple silver frame, about four inches by six, which cradled a color photo of the two of them smiling and holding hands. It was gone.

He'd never really noticed how much power certain things have, she looked around his house to see the things that could be removed without him even knowing. There were a few paintings on the walls, and knick-knacks on shelves, that he would probably never even miss. Even the TV in the living room could be gone for days without him noticing. That is, until he sat down to watch a show. He never realized that that photo was the thing he'd miss the minute it was gone. He wondered if the world would miss him, but he didn't wonder long. He knew the small picture frame spot on the dresser, the one void of dust—Pledge-shiny waxed—held more power and created a deeper sense of loss than anything he would ever be capable of in his life. He was useless and wouldn't be missed.

His clothes removed, he walked naked into the living room. He checked the rope that he had tied to the table, and then he gently tied the other end about his neck. As he did so he looked out the window and directly into the eyes of a large pink ape. The wind turned the great helium head in his direction and the ape's eyes reflected nothing of him or the room. He had already disappeared as far as this monster was concerned. If it showed any interest in him at all, it was probably as an apartment hunter looking for a safe place to store its deflated self until the next parade. He walked to the window and opened it wide. If it was

loud before, it was now a thunderous din, like a drunken giant's calliope. Laughter and goodwill rushed up from the street, over the sash, and coursed their merry notes across his body. He could hear children screaming—their joy-filled voices painfully making him imagine candy-coated smiles. It also made him realize how far away he was. The rope was a touch rough around his throat so he untied it and went to find something soft. It might clutter the body a bit, lose the dramatic "found nude" headline, but, chafing was chafing, and there was no reason to be uncomfortable.

He walked back to his bedroom and noticed his dresser was as it should be. On the way to it, he paused and listened to a tune from below. It was a parade song, nothing you'd ever listen to in the car, but every time he heard it, he enjoyed the song more. *Why couldn't he be ready now*, he thought, *this would be a great piece to swing to; it had a really nice beat.*

A few of Katherine's things were left over from her departure, including a scarf that he'd found in the back seat of his car. He'd stowed it in a dresser drawer, the one he was opening now, and there it was, lying across a row of neatly folded T-shirts. The scarf was a light sky blue with bits of bright yellow and green. It was too bright for this room now, although he did not remember the colors standing out when she wore it—funny how things change. The scarf still smelled like her. He wondered why perfume stayed on clothes longer than it stayed on skin, and how, even washed, like his button-down grey shirt had been, perfume could stay unfaithfully familiar as it clung to the cloth. And maybe, there was that, his infidelity, but wasn't that the right of all men? Hell, he took her tears and her monthly moods, why couldn't she accept him?

Wild horns now crazily brayed from outside, just as he thought, it was *them*. He peered out the window and a gang of clowns was below—reckless in the street, dancing and honking, frightening the children. He pulled the window closed for a second and, as wood touched sill, he shut his eyes and thought back to an unpleasant time—a car ride with Katherine that had gone sour. What was she trying to say as he yelled at her—her voice-empty, tear-touched lips, talking without sound while the horns from the cars behind were pushing him, forcing his rage? He had heard the voices of those behind though, or at least the man in the first car—the crying pussy screaming as he was pulled through his window and beaten down in the street. What nerve, telling him to move on. And those other horn honking pricks, the ones who had hastily reversed their cars as he came toward them, he heard *them* all right. And he *was* sorry, as he climbed back in his car, carrying with him the aggression of the moment. Yes, he'd shoved her. Yes, he hit hard enough to knock her out, but it was really just a push that had gotten out of control, and if the window and the door jam hadn't been there to rudely stop her head, things would've been fine.

The clowns moved on down the street and, except for the occasional brassy squeal that they had left behind, he quickly forgot them. He tied the silk scarf around his neck and then gently laid the rope upon it. *Ahhhhhh*, that was better, and the knot probably had a smarter look, not being laid on bare skin. He coiled the rope in his hand and then climbed up to the window and worked his way into a sitting position on the sill. There he was sitting, feeling the breeze, and noticing that bare rumps were not made for rough sills. He sat a while, dangling his legs over the unknowing crowd, listening to the sounds of the street, and waiting for a possible telephone ring from inside. Katherine had been a touch telepathic sometimes, almost as if she were following him, the way she read his face. So maybe, even now—although he was not in any great despair—she might reach out to send her goodbyes.

A float rounded the corner, this time a cartoon bear that he failed to recognize. It took up quite a bit of street as it lumbered and danced in a non-threatening bear-type manner. That was Katherine's pet name for him, her "bear" or her "big bear." Yes, bears could be like this one, smiling, toddling giant cuteness down city streets, or, they could be like other bears, like he was sometimes. He let the rope drop. It took a clear fall, not tangling itself on any poles or parapets, and then he leaned forward, with his hands at his side, ready to spring out toward the street. He wanted to wait—let the happy bear have its day, and then he'd jump during the next band. After a momentary stall—something wasn't moving on the corner of Main and 12th—the parade rolled on. The great bear moved down the block, and the One-hundred and Eleventh Street School Band came along below the window. They were wonderful—black and purple uniforms, orange plumed feather hats. He pushed out from the sill and fell the distance left of the thirty-two foot rope. He caught right above the windows on the first floor and his head snapped back with a loud, clean pop. He bounced once or twice against the wall and then he came to rest—beautiful colored streamers fell and hung festively over his body. They matched the scarf perfectly, and as he died his legs twitched and kicked in time with the band.

The Extraction

"She's a sociopath, a murdering sociopath and she's taken my heart!"

His office was small—the standard shrink setup—a big couch, an overstuffed chair, boxes of Kleenex, and a wall covered with, "here's-how-to-fix-his-head," books. But there was nothing on those shelves to solve my problem—my heart had been violently, and with little regret, ripped from my chest.

"Jack, please," my therapist was using his best sooth-the-beast tones. "Calm down, please."

"You don't get it, *Robert*." I was crying, sarcastic and screaming at the same time. "She's got my heart! She's got my fucking heart!"

"Okay, okay," he tried reasoning. "First off, that's a figure of speech; she doesn't *really* have your heart. You're emotionally attached to her and you're upset—rightfully so."

I grabbed the front of my blood-soaked shirt and ripped it open, exposing the jagged hole beneath. "Look at this! Am I lying? She cut me and she took it. She fucking took it."

"Jack, please. If she took your heart you'd be dead, but you're not dead, you're here screaming at me; you're alive, you're very much alive."

He was incapable of seeing it, but he worked on a sliding scale, and I was broke.

"Here," he said as he handed me a large blue pill and a paper cup half filled with water. "Take this, please, it'll help."

I grabbed the pill from his hand and swallowed it dry. I wanted him to see it fall past the hole in my chest, but instead, it got caught in my throat and I was forced to drink—bitter, inner-city tap water.

"I can help you," he said. "But first you need to relax, calm down. I'll help you get it back."

"Don't humor me!" I yelled. "And don't act like you can't see it." I gestured wildly at my shirt. "You know it's gone. Look! Look at it!"

"Jack, I believe that you believe, and right now that's a start. Can you just listen to me, please, and relax?"

He got up and pulled the shades closed. I waited to stop breathing—this was agony. "Sometimes," he said, "and I'm not saying that this is true in your case, but sometimes people can become so upset that they actually convince themselves—and their vision—that they're seeing and experiencing things that, well, just aren't so."

I ran my hand over the hole in my chest as he talked—I played with the front of my bloody shirt as I watched him. I gently tapped and pushed my fingers into the hollow as he pontificated—he was an idiot.

"Why don't you tell me how it happened then?" He asked. "Tell me *how* she took your heart."

I sat back on the couch and tried to calm down. I *was* losing a lot of blood, and I don't know if the pill he gave me was kicking in, but I figured that if I calmly told him, laid out the story, he might take me seriously and take notice of the hole.

"It was last night," I began, "we were supposed to go out, but she said she had homework to finish—math, she needed it done by tomorrow. I didn't trip on it, she was in school and a lot more conscientious than I'd ever been, so I waited around looking at porn for a bit and then I drove over to her house. I told you she got that place in Long Beach, near the gay ghetto, right? Well, parking's a real bitch down there so when I pulled up, I didn't see her car out front, but I'd texted her and she said she was home, so I drove around a while and finally found a spot on Falcon—a couple blocks over from her place. It was a short walk, but along the way I got a taste of how a single girl might feel. I had to cruise by those boy bars on Broadway—had the leather cats calling me names and trying to get me to hang out for a drink. Anyway, I got to her house and knocked on the door. She didn't answer. Now, I'd come a bit earlier than she wanted, but what the fuck, I figured I'd just read or something. I hadn't told her I was on my way, so I texted again and asked how it was going. She got right back to me, LOL about how she was lying around in the living room with her britches off as she studied.

Well, now *I knew she was lying*, she wasn't home because I was knocking. The fucking bitch had no idea I was standing at her front door—so I broke in."

"What?" Dr. Robert was shocked. "Did you just say that you broke into her apartment?"

"No," I replied. "I didn't *'break in'*; I took a screen off and went through the window. I didn't kick the fucking door down."

"You committed a crime, Jack." "Yeah," I grabbed at my bloodsoaked shirt. "Well, I don't think *she's* going to be pressing charges, is she?"

The doctor sighed and waved his hand for more of the story. I threw him a disgusted don't-stop-me-again look, and then I gave it to him.

"Her house was a mess—clothes and books all over the place. She's gorgeous, but she's a fucking slob—her car looks like a homeless camp. Anyway, I was quiet going in, just in case she *was* home and, if so, I was gonna pull one of those 'look-at-the-cute-burglar-boyfriend' things, but she wasn't there, so after a quick look around I went through her things, or at least I started to, because when I got to her bedroom, I glanced at the bed and there were rope ties out—one on each corner, with handcuffed leather attachments and a big dildo lying on the mattress. Now you know I got a bit of the kink running through me, but we've never fucked around like that, so unless she had something planned for later, this wasn't meant for me."

Dr. Robert broke in. "Why didn't you just leave? You and I have talked about this before. You know she's unfaithful, always has been. You could've been arrested. What are you getting out of this?"

"I'M GETTING THE FUCKING TRUTH OUT OF IT!" I screamed, "I want to see her doing it. Every time I think I catch

27

her doing something there's always an explanation, always a reason that what I'm seeing isn't true."

The doctor cut me off, "she admitted…"

"SHE NEVER ADMITTED ANYTHING! She cries and rolls those sad brown eyes at me—she's a witch, a sociopathic witch!"

"Jack?"

"No, not Jack. You listen to me. I got a text as I was standing by the bed. It was her, asking me if I'd left home yet. I was quick. I wrote back 'no' and asked if she was done studying. She wrote back telling me that she was gonna take a nap and that the phone would be off for a bit, so I should take my time coming over. You see, she always does that, always has a reason why she can't answer, and why I can't get a hold of her. So I throw a quick 'yeah, no problem babe, I'm bummed I gotta wait, but let me know when you're up.' I threw that last bit in because if she thought I went along too easily she'd get suspicious. So, I didn't have a real plan or anything, but I knew my car was cool, because like I said, it was a couple blocks over, so I sat there, kind of whimpered for a bit, and then tried to put a thought together."

The doctor broke in, "We've talked about this before, you taking a moment out—running the situation through your head—and then, maybe calling a friend, or myself; and at least leaving that very illegal situation."

28

"Yeah, and I probably could have. I was deep, but I *was* calming down—having a real moment of clarity—realizing that I didn't need to deal with this shit, just like you've said. I *was* better than her, *and* better than this—but then I heard voices in the alley. It was her, and she was laughing, so I got inside the closet."

"What?" The doctor was taken aback.

"I would have climbed under the bed but it was full of boxes and shit, dirty clothes, shoes. The closet wasn't much better, but it was easier, and I figured if she needed something she'd just grab it off the floor. So there I was, standing in a crowd of empty coats and dresses, when I heard 'em come in—two people, as far as I could tell, her and some woman, and it was real weird because I heard laughter, talking, and then silence, laughter, talking, silence, like somebody was pressing the 'mute' button during their conversation and then they'd start right up again. I was tripping, but then I realized that they must have been kissing. I couldn't see 'em, but the silence, followed by the talking, told me they were. Fuck, I wanted to break out and confront 'em right then—come out real Bruce Lee style—kicking and throwing blows, but not this time. Fortunately, I realized I had done that before, it didn't work." You've caught her with someone before?" The doctor was quizzical. "You never told me that."

"No! Fuck! I didn't say I *caught her! I've* never caught her, *but I've caught her* getting ready to do shit, and I broke in before she did it, so I didn't actually catch her."

29

"So, you haven't actually caught her being unfaithful?"

"STOP IT!" I yelled. "YOU FUCKING SOUND LIKE HER! NO, that's what I told you." I spoke to him slowly now, "*I needed evidence. I needed to catch her. That's why I stayed.*"

Doctor Robert gave me a disbelieving look that I verbally rolled right over. "I was good. I didn't yell out, watched my breathing, stayed calm and I waited—just like you've taught me."

"I never taught you that," the doctor spoke. "I taught you to leave." Again I ignored him—he needed to be quiet.

"They screwed around in the kitchen a bit, her and whomever— and it started to look like I was gonna have to just come out and confront them, but then they walked in. God, that *thing* she was kissing, who sounded like a woman? It didn't look like one. I peeped out through the closet door—just a touch, a crack. The bitch had a fucking chain wallet, and Levi's cuffed over her boots. I'm telling you, a real nasty-looking thing with dreadlocked dirty blonde hair hanging past her shoulders. She had her back to me, and my girl had her arms thrown around the bitch's neck like some lesbian perfume ad—her face buried in what I assumed to be this thing's tits. I wouldn't be surprised if that big bitch had 'em taped down or whacked off or whatever—I mean, for all intents and purposes, this could have been a soft-assed ugly boy. I stayed quiet, and they kissed, and then that big girl laid my chick down on the bed where she started pulling and stroking those rope ties as they made out—

like she was stroking a cock or something, the way she pulled on 'em. Well, then they separated—broke it off—and the big girl got up and started taking off her clothes—folding them actually, which was kind of funny because the floor was littered with piles of used shirts and shit. It would have made more sense if she just tossed her crap on the ground. She took off her pants and T-shirt, and then she pulled off this sports bra and these big britches—more like a man's BVD's—bigger than mine. Then she stands there, naked, except for that underwear and her nasty-looking wig hair, and she watches my girl as *she* begins taking off *her* things and throwing them on the floor."

"How far were you going to let this go?" The doctor asked.

"I told you, Doc, all the way. I had to see it, but I *was* a bit scared, wondering if I could physically take on that big bitch when I came out of the closet—but I didn't need to worry about that. My girl had pulled off all her things and then she started squirming and wiggling around on that bed like a viper, nesting on the covers, and that big old dyke, well she had her hands down the front of her big panties, like she was rubbing that nasty snatch of hers as she watched my girl move. And then Doc, my girl holds out a hand, reaching for that mannish thing, and she grabs onto her and with crazy strength, my chick pulled that bitch down on the bed and flipped her over so now she's lying on her back with my girl on top, straddling her, holding her down. Fuck, that big girl wasn't pretty at all, hell, she wasn't even cute—more like a beast than a girl—and I was almost jealous that my chick was about to have sex with her but then I remembered that unless that dyke had an 8-inch clit there wasn'tany real fucking going on… do you think that's weird?"

"What?" Dr. Robert was confused. "Do I think what's weird?"

"Do you think it's weird that I don't really think it's cheating because she doesn't have a cock?"

"I don't get it. What are you saying? Are you saying she's not cheating on you?"

"I don't know. Maybe I just use that to lessen the pain." I touched the hole in my chest, "Not that it helps much.

"Anyway, so my girl grabs one of those ties and locks that dyke's right arm up, and then the left arm, and then each leg—I thought the ropes were for my chick, not the big girl. When my girl had her all tied up, she started sliding on her, grinding her cunt against her like she's sitting on a cock, riding her, and then she reaches down on the side of the bed, grabs a big black hood and pulls it over the big girl's head. That big dyke didn't like it—she was jerking around, trying to get away, struggling hard, but then my girl leaned toward her and said, *'You go quiet now.'* Just like that, and that big old bitch just laid her head back— relaxed and silent—like an animal hypnotized into sleep."

"Okay, okay," Dr. Robert stopped me. "God damn it, Jack,

that's enough. I told you before; *it's a waste of my time and yours for you to keep coming in here with these crazy tales…*" He started to get up.

"No, please, Robert, listen to me. Please, I'm not lying. Let me finish. Please!" I begged him; *so maybe I had fucked with him once or twice, but not this time*—I was telling the truth.

"I know it sounds crazy, but she did it, and that big girl looked like she was knocked out—lying there, not moving. I'm wondering if she's even breathing, and then out of nowhere, my girl cocked her arm back and punched her in the face—an undefended shot I knew did damage. And then she threw another, blow after blow. I could hear the cracking bone, the flesh tearing. She was beating that girl of hers with more fury than I'd ever seen and she was yelling, screaming, '*I hate you! I fucking hate you!*' It was sickening, and I was terrified. She was beating on her—screaming, crying, pounding, on that big girl who just laid there knocked out, taking hit after hit, and then I saw the blood seeping from under the hood, staining the bed, covering my girl's hands, and I couldn't take it anymore. I broke out of that closet and I screamed: STOP IT! FUCKING STOP IT!

"She stopped. My girl froze mid-punch—arm pulled back like a cocked trigger flash—a beautifully vicious beast held at bay. And then she turned on me with eyes driven by checked fury, and she smiled—a great big alligator smile that sent waves of perfumed terror rippling across my soul, and she whispered to me the same line she whispered before, '*You go quiet now.*' And I did. I stood there, rooted to the floor, arms to my side, eyes open and fully aware, unable to move—a coma standing in a crowded closet."

"So, what happened?" The doctor asked, a touch of belief creeping into his voice. "What did she do then?"

"She looked happy to see me—like she wasn't doing anything wrong at all. Her smile turned into a summer afternoon walk, and with a two-lovers-cuddled-at-home grin she reached down and lovingly squeezed my crotch as she said, '*Do you like watching me? You're a naughty little boy aren't you?*' If only I had sensation to react to her words you'd have seen the fear run winter cold on my arms—she was not human.

"She slid her hand up my body, like a child sailing a dream ship on a nighttime river, and then she docked her fingers at my lips and told me to wait, wait for her. And, as though I had a choice, I stood there and watched as she untied her lover and cared for her wounds. She removed the hood from the big girl—whose face was swollen and colored red with blood. But the big dyke didn't move—leaving me to wonder if she was dead, but she wasn't. With a word, a soft-mouthed word from my girl her beaten lover arose and dressed herself in trancelike, mechanical-girl movements. With abused precision she donned her clothes and then walked from the room. I was still held in state so I couldn't see the exchange as my girl followed her out, but I heard the front door close and her returning footsteps.

"Then she came over to where I was standing. *'What am I to do with you?'* She asked—still holding that sweet lover's tone. *'You are a naughty one, but I like naughty, and you stopped my fun.'* She grabbed me by the collar of my shirt, her dainty hand wrapped, cuddled in the cloth, and then she pulled me toward the bed. I followed. She spun me 'round and then unbuttoned my pants, sliding them off my hips and kneeling before me—a submissive pose but one more akin to eating the soft belly of a kill than it was to kneeling before her master. She put her hands on my ass and I felt her fingernails cutting deep into my flesh—although there was no pain accompanying their assault—it was as if my body was made of wax, a man-doll for her to play with. I felt myself get hard and then she opened her mouth and swallowed me deep, but I received no pleasure from her, no great sensation at her touch. It was just wet and cold, almost as if I was exposed to the outside—a winter mouth devoid of warmth. She then stood, pulled my shirt over my head, and pushed me backwards onto the bed that was recently vacated by her lover. She pulled off my shoes, my pants, and then reused the ties on me. I was now straddled on my back, across the bed, with my cock erect to her will."

"Jack?" the doctor's voice was soft, almost reverent, "You're bleeding." He pointed at my shirt.

35

"Yes," I calmly replied. "I know." He really was beginning to see, but I wasn't about to stop.

"She stepped up onto the bed, stood with her bare feet on the mattress, and looked down on me. From where I lay she was a giantess, legs spread, hovering over me. She touched herself, her fingers sensually caressing the outside of her cunt before she reached inside. I was not a man to her, just property waiting to be scented. And then she squatted over me and placed my hard unfeeling cock inside and rode me until I guess I came. I wasn't conscious of any real release, but she seemed satisfied, completed. She stayed squat—inhaling deeply, sucking her stomach in, drawing the semen up into her womb and rubbing her pelvic mound in wide circular moves as she repeated my name."

"Did she want a child?" the doctor asked. "Had you talked about it, was it discussed before?"

"No," I told him. "She'd mentioned a family, but there were no real plans. She climbed off me and then lay at my side—again, soft and loving, nestled against my skin. It was a posture she'd assumed many times, but that was before I knew what she was."

"What do you mean?" he asked. "What was she?"

"She was a witch—able to control and seduce her lovers to the point of their extinction. She placed trances and spells, wove lies with truth, love with selfishness. This is a woman who would've been fuel for a fire—accelerant on a medieval pyre. She was a devil; a demon with a cunt that held the comfort of an evening slumber and a kiss like an early morning mist drifting upon an ocean of forgetfulness.

"She put her lips to my forehead, and spoke: '*I hate myself for wanting her.*' She gestured outside, in what I took as the general direction of her beaten lover. '*She means nothing to me; it's you I love. That woman, and the others I've had who are like her, they're just shadows of me, totems of my sexuality I rape and deface.*'

"I couldn't protest, or argue with her, I was still trapped in that space of evil compliance."

I took a few shallow breaths, and then went back to my story.

"She continued her explanation: *'I can't stay with you now—not after you've seen this, and I'm going to kill this child before he's born.'* She tenderly touched her stomach. *'His death will be my punishment, the promise of you that I've ripped from my life.'* She was tracing her fingers over my heart as she spoke. I could feel her tugging at my skin, like pulling a loose nail from a finger, or the torn head of a blister off your foot. Tears welled up in my eyes because I didn't understand. If I was so important to her, caused her so much pain, how could she do this? How could she hurt me?"

"You were everything to me," she said, *"and you promised me your heart—your love forever."*

"And I *had* done that. I promised that I'd love her, and my heart was hers. *'I'm taking what you owe me,'* she purred, *'I'm taking what's mine, and then I'm leaving.'* There was nothing I could say. "It was then that my body dipped below the surface, like an old wooden coaster plunging helplessly toward the ground. I felt my heart rise from my chest and then I blacked out. When I came to, the room was empty. I was lying on the floor of her now-vacant place and I was without a heart. She was gone. "it's quite frightening to know that what supposedly drives blood

38

through your veins, the engine of life that tirelessly pumps throughout the day, can be cut from your body and you can still exist. As you might imagine, I was turned away from the emergency room. That was my first stop after I wandered dazed from her apartment to my car. The doctors there couldn't see the problem either. They seemed busy and in no mood to listen, so I came to you. I know you can't help me. You can't replace what she took, but maybe now you can acknowledge the hole, see how the blood refuses to dry on my shirt, and watch how I live devoid of her presence."

"Jack, there must be something I can do," the doctor said sympathetically.

"You could kill her," I laughed, only half joking. "But if I were you, I'd be afraid that maybe one day she might come here with a different tale, a twist on what I just told you, a gleam in her eye as she sits on your sofa and makes *you* feel warm and loved."

"She'd never do that," he said. "Of course she would. You've helped me, and now you believe she did this to me because I loved her. A true witch can't suffer a love to live."

I leaned back on his sofa. I was tired, worn down and through.

"Jack?" He spoke in a kind voice. "I'm afraid your time is up."

"Yes," I said, "I know."

I took one last breath as the hole in my chest devoured me.

Untamed

Animals can be tamed, so can men, but underneath the fur or the business suit, the bejeweled collar or that perfect tie—dangerously held in place, is the wild nature of the beast. Sometimes this nature can be held down long enough to drown under the socialized weight of the modern world, but at other times the true animal lies fiercely kicking beneath the skin—waiting for a chance to surface and catch its breath.

The teen boy was wild—at least that's what he looked like to the Outsider—wild and dangerous, unstable, the kind of boy who might do anything in a crowd. The Outsider pulled his jacket closed and one-hand checked his wallet. He hoped there weren't more of these boys.

"Hey man, you got some change?" The boy's eyes drifted to the recently covered wallet pocket.

"I'm sorry, no," the Outsider nervously rattled. "I, I only have plastic." He was polite, but dishonest.

"You sure you don't have nothing?" The boy asked as he monkey-cocked his head to one side. He was tall, white, his jet-black hair matching the black leather coat on his back. He sported a white T-shirt and straight-legged Levi's cuffed over boots—'50s motorcycle grease-boy look—the kind of Marlon

Brando cool that the Outsider wished he could summon up on a Friday night, but he just couldn't.

"How 'bout a ride then?" The boy asked. "I heard keys. You got a car, yeah?"

The Outsider had a car. He also had a wife, two children, a large mortgage and a small paying job. The Outsider had lots of things.

"Come on man," the boy continued, "it ain't far, but I missed the fucking bus. I'm gonna be late."

The Outsider could have easily brushed the boy off and limp-dicked his way to the car, but for some reason he paused, as if something instinctual yet foreign had just crawled out and

42

gently wrapped itself around his legs... he became ashamed to say no to the boy.

"Okay, I guess so, if it's not too far." He submissively led the boy toward the car.

The wild boy was cool as he climbed in and sat back in the worn leather seat. It was one of the few new-car options that the Outsider didn't take a pass on—leather had seemed *right*. The boy fooled with the window button as the Outsider looked down and unconsciously admired the outline of the boy's cock through his pants. It was large, well shaped, and looked heavy. The Outsider had a cock once—when he was a teen he had a real nice piece. He was proud of the way it stood forth in the shower, how it hung down between his legs as he walked, but not any more. He couldn't remember the last time he felt proud. He reached down and tried to adjust what he had left—the beige poly-cotton blend of his slacks city-boy whimpered then laid still.

"Cool car man," the boy said. "What's it cost, a car like this? You must have some job, huh?"

The Outsider felt slightly buoyed by the boy's praise of his mid-priced mist grey sedan, until he spotted a grape juice stain and the gummed end of a Zwieback cookie on the seat. He tried to brush it down casually. *"Fucking Sheila, I told her not to let the kids eat in the car."*

The boy repeated, rolled on with his praise. "Yeah, real cool ride. You must have a good job, you a lawyer or something?"

The Outsider nodded his head with a move that could easily be mistaken for a casual yes. It was another lie, the Outsider was a process server, and he knew his car was shit.

"Hey, pull over here," the boy pointed to a run-down corner market. "I gotta get me something."

The Outsider didn't remember any such store near his work and, on second glance, he realized that without paying attention he had driven the boy farther and deeper into an area that the Outsider had no business being in. It was certainly nowhere he'd drift into on his own. He hesitantly pulled to the curb and the boy jumped out without shutting the door. The Outsider called after him in a weak voice, "Hey, not too long, huh?"

The boy didn't answer and the Outsider leaned over and

hurredly pulled the door closed. He glanced out the front windshield and was not happy about the black street corner animals lounging in twos and threes against the faded paint walls of the building. He knew about those people, shiftless, lazy, drug dealers all, they weren't to be trusted—and this was no place to be alone. He felt unprotected, vulnerable, almost as if something might come along and rip his arm off. He turned the radio on, but for some reason the reception was shit. It sounded distant—far off—even the commercials that were normally twice as loud as the soft adult-oriented pop he enjoyed seemed garbled and washed out. He felt lonely and wished the boy would return. The kid was smaller, much younger, and technically weaker than the Outsider, but even at six-foot-four, two hundred and thirty pounds, the Outsider felt small. Sensing the boy's experience, he felt safe in his presence. His thoughts drifted to the wife he had at home...

Sheila had always thought him weak. Yeah, maybe she'd never come right out and said it, but, it was there, neatly tucked inside her wifely tones. He knew that she thought she could've done better, and he'd seen the way she looked at check-stand Tom— the tall, attractive grocery store manager, who had a full head of hair and looked like he might work out. One night, after she'd talked him into a "gotta-get-something-from-the-store," run, he

caught her sizing him up in the car, looking disappointed as she slowly ran her buyer's-remorse eyes over his bargain goods— the thinning hair and softening gut of a somewhat past-the-

expiration-date man. He watched as she shook off the thought of him, and turned her mind toward what he imagined must have been Tom. He saw her face break into that slow, soft, upturned, nasty little grin that meant she was mind fucking that overgrown box boy. He knew what she was doing, and it was okay, he had a fantasy of his own—a late-night store run that didn't work out so well for the check-out man—a fantasy that ended with big Tom knocked out and burbling in the Outsider's piss. But, of course, it was just a fantasy, and it scared him now to even think of it. The one time he had met Tom's eyes across the checkout counter—even though the manager was store-bought-customer-polite—the Outsider had quailed beneath his glance. It was as if Tom could read his thoughts and he was about to be pummeled and dropped for his insolence...

The car door quickly re-opened and the wild boy jumped in with a six-pack of cold beer and an even cooler grin of frosty-beaded satisfaction.

'Come on, hit it!" the boy ordered, "Motherfucker... ha, crazy, fucking bitch."

The Outsider, without looking, wildly accelerated, forcing the car into traffic. "You gotta love these yellow motherfuckers, ha! What the fuck did he think he was gonna do? Standing up all

shit like that." The boy was talking loudly to himself, but not being clear;

46

babbling disjointed commentary on what might have been some sort of violent exchange, and now, even louder, his voice rose into a sing-songy gay yellow squeal. "You're bleeding on me! You're bleeding on me!"

The boy was laughing, head thrown back against the seat, great white teeth bared and reflecting the hard flesh of his lips—he was exhilarated from his exchange. It was then the Outsider caught a look at the boy's hands. There were fresh cuts on his knuckles—red top coating on Levi caressing fingers. The Outsider could smell the blood, and it thrilled him.

When Sheila bled it was always such a turnoff—that is, when she'd let him in the bed. He never slept with her when she was menstruating, it was dirty, gross, but the blood on this boy's knuckles was like flipping through the pages of a triple X magazine—he was a child fascinated by the unrepentant naughtiness of the ragged skin.

It was then that the Outsider really began to shift, and what had seeped in earlier started to slowly overtake the tamed man—he began to change. The boy glanced over and smiled at the new lustful countenance of the Outsider, and then he took his cut hand and held it back-knuckled under the man's nose, teasing him, before he drug it slowly along his cheek, marking him with scent. The Outsider leaned into it and without thought, kitten-purred tragically against the boy's torn hand—bonding with the more experienced male—and as the boy started to pull away, the Outsider grabbed his arm, and drew the boy's fingers back toward his mouth. He reached out with his tongue and licked the blood off the boy's hand.

"Ha, it's good, huh? Too bad it's mine." The boy was pleased. "Never hit a fucker in the mouth—dirty fucking teeth, man. It's fun to feel 'em break, but they got dirty teeth," the boy laughed as he spoke. The Outsider became impatient. He wanted to be let in on the action, and like a hungry whelp, he barked at the boy. "What happened?" the Outsider demanded. The boy swung around heavy, pushing the question down with his raised body and aggressive posture. The Outsider quickly backed off, symbolically rolled over in the seat, and talked slowly, using the proper respect.

"I mean," the Outsider began again, "are you okay?"

The boy cut the Outsider slack he hadn't yet earned. "We needed beverages man," the boy laughingly mimicked a low, drugged-out, stoner voice, from a popular film that the Outsider had once watched with his wife. *He remembered Sheila putting up a stink about the film's foul language and sexual innuendo, but he didn't care now.* The boy held up a beer, took a long, slow jungle pull off the suds, and then passed the half emptied can to the Outsider, who greedily put his mouth over the tombstone opening, swallowing the boy's scent and chasing it

"He fucking tried to stop me, man—walking out with a couple down with cold malt.of cold beers and all five-foot-two of grass-hoppin' shit comes 'round the counter acting all Kung-Fu bad," the boy slid back to the sing-songy yellow jive. "Hey man, you got pay! You got pay!"

"When he grabbed for the beer I just swung it up and hit him in the face with it. Then I tee'd off on that big ole fucking head of his—knocked his ass out."

"Really?" asked the Outsider incredulously.

"*Yeah, really.*" The Boy held up his cut hand. "What the fuck?" He flung blood on the Outsider's face. "You think I'm fuckin' with you?"

"No, I just…"

"Fuckin' A, man," the boy cheered. "Right in the fucking mouth!"

The Outsider wished he could have seen it, or better yet, maybe *he* could have given the little yellow man a kick—hit him when he was down, maybe a bit more… he wondered what it was like to hit someone.

"I got cash, too," the boy held up a wad of crumpled bills. "I mean, fuck, with him all sleeping on the job and everything, there ain't no sense not getting in that register and teaching him a lesson for being so damn lazy." The boy fanned the cash like a child waving an exemplary school report.

"Gas money, baby!" He held out a twenty to the Outsider. "Go ahead, take it man."

The Outsider looked at the boy's outstretched hand and then tentatively, like a cautious child, reached toward the bill.

"Come on," the boy coaxed. "It's cool."

The Outsider took the money. It felt good to be part of; it was freeing, yet inclusive at the same time. He was looking forward to spending the cash.

The boy and the Outsider now slow-cruised the town—the boy pointing out dangers, and easy meats, things to avoid, and places to dig in. The Outsider was hungry for knowledge and listened rabidly as he drove. This was a city he was unfamiliar with; a world he knew existed but had no idea of the breadth and color of the land. And, as they drove, he grew. The Outsider's hips felt heavier and his shoulders rolled slightly forward.

****

"You gotta watch for Felix, this is his place." The boy pointed to an alley separating two old apartment buildings. "Gave me my first cut, that nasty fucker." The boy pulled up his shirt displaying a long jagged scar running across the length of his stomach. "Took my cash, and then cut me," the boy giggled. The Outsider lifted his face, inhaling the air as he strained to catch a whiff of Felix's scent so he might know it if he came by again—a cut like that was serious, nothing to laugh at.

The boy looked the Outsider over, reappraising his size and possible worth, and then he flashed an idea. "Pull back here," the boy directed the Outsider to a small dirty parking lot around the corner from the alley. "We're gonna do this. He don't know you."

The Outsider was clueless, but the wild boy fired off a quick plan—a way in, but as far as the Outsider could see it, no real goal of completion, just a roll-up attack, using the Outsider as bait.

"He'll never see you coming—no offense man, but you look like a stupid fuck. You lose that jacket and tie and you're just one more coked-out junior exec hoping for a downtown score."

The Outsider nodded his head in agreement and when ordered, stripped down to his shirt, shoes, and pants. And then, after an extremely weak, "Hey, those just cost me," objection, his tie and jacket were tossed from the car. He was ready.

It was a city street much like any other, but the Outsider could almost sense the cast-off bones and various body parts invisibly strewn about the alley lair of Felix. It was a dangerous place. The building on the right, a great rock cliff, to the left, a brick wall running from the floor of the city into the stars. Light steam and a gutter stench of river drifted on the air from the alley opening—the haze of an inner city plain. The Outsider walked up, feigning preoccupation—a human waterbuck searching for sweeter grass in the alley. Felix was there. The Outsider could feel the heavy weight of his presence; the polyester wrapped crocodile, fat and dangerous, leaning against the hard alley wall. And then, that deep Latin hiss of a voice...

"You looking for something, bitch?"

Felix moved toward the center of the alley—strong coiled action, low smooth and vicious cool. The Outsider felt his balls drop and he deeply inhaled the wicked scent of abused flesh and alcohol-raped breath. Felix was beautiful. He was scarred and used, chewed up by the city, yes, but before it could swallow him, he'd been spit back as spun hard sugar into the street. His face was cut brown dirt. His eyes, blue Cadillac Deville, and in his mouth the glint of spit-shined gold. He hypnotized the Outsider.

"I said you looking for something?"

"Coke?" The Outsider stammered—it was more question than request. The Outsider played his part well. Felix wide-smiled

52

across the alley and stepped closer to the man. "I ain't even gonna ask if you're a cop. You too stupid to be a cop. And there ain't no sense in selling what I ain't got, and you ain't getting. Now why don't you reach in those fucking pockets and dump your shit on the ground."

The Outsider backed into the alley, away from the entrance, further into darkness, away from the street; and Felix followed. The alley dweller was looking forward to a midafternoon snack of credit cards, wallet, and watch.

"I said drop your shit, bitch. "Felix flashed his claws—a blade, pulled from the air, clicked and switched in his hand.

The wild boy now silently entered the alley—quiet, jungle-stealth calm—advancing on Felix, as Felix advanced on the Outsider. In his hand, the boy held a board, a large piece of cast-off alley trash waiting to be used. The Outsider stopped

53

retreating, reached into his pockets, and made like he was about to surrender his worth.

"Yeah, dat's right big man. You got nowheres to go, and maybe ole Felix is gonna give you something to suck on while you're here." Felix reached down and lovingly stroked his cock. "Shit, you prolly didn't even come down for blow; you come down here to get on my shit."

He pulled foul-breath close to the Outsider, and it was then that the boy struck—a flash lightening blow to the side of Felix's head. A swing, climaxed with a thick thundercloud thud crushing the beast's skull—rendering the monster useless, knife clattered to the street, cock, withering in his pants. Felix staggered, blindly slow-danced toward the Outsider and the boy took another swing. This time the blow landed squarely on the brute's face—crushing bone, splitting flesh. What was left of Felix collapsed to the ground. The boy dragged the body behind a dumpster and then turned and handed the wooden tool to the Outsider.

"Here you go, get some. But be quick."

The Outsider grabbed the board and tentatively poked the body with it. The already decaying flesh of the beast gave in, then out, manipulated breath by the Outsider's touch. He wasn't sure what to do.

"Go on," the boy urged. "What are you waiting for? Hit the fucker. We gotta get out of here." The Outsider handed back the club. "But, I don't feel mad," he said.

"Mad?" The boy was shocked. "What the fuck did you just say?" "I don't feel mad," repeated the Outsider. "I kind of wanna hit him, I mean it seems like the right thing to do, but I don't feel mad."

"Mad, about what?" The boy asked, "I don't get it. How you gonna be mad at that?" He pointed to the body. "There's him and you, me, those people out there," the boy gestured to the street. "We do what we do. It's got nothing to do with 'mad.' What the fuck you talking about?"

The Outsider could almost get what the boy was saying—his simple, street animal logic was walking along the edges of a mind made soft by the teachings of weak men—men who thought they were above something, created by something, to be more than men. The Boy now jokingly questioned the corpse: "What's up now, bitch? Who's cut now, huh, fucker?"

The Outsider followed the questions as if he expected Felix to answer—he didn't. The boy turned to him, once again he held up the wood. "You sure?" The Outsider began to move, reached for the plank, but hesitated.

"That's okay man," the boy dropped the wood to the ground. "You'll get a taste for it soon enough."

The boy rifled Felix's pockets, scored a small bag of dope and a few large bills, and then threw a parting kick at what used to be a most dangerous man, before he turned to leave. The Outsider tagged along for a few yards, but then, right before they reached the entrance to the alley, he had a non-thought and ran back and stomped on the body. It was a quick, non-remorseful, non-enlightened move, which brought him praise from the boy, and as the Outsider walked back toward his instructor, he stopped, bent over, and picked up one of Felix's teeth—the spit-shined gold incisor.

The Outsider held the tooth in his palm and smiled a big man smile, before he stuffed it in his pocket, and hustled to catch up with the wild boy.

****

"You stand behind me, when we go in," the boy explained

56

protocol to the Outsider. "Prolly get beat down if you walked in first, and keep your fucking mouth shut, these guys don't like new things, and you're real new."

They had jumped on the Interstate and had gotten off a few short exits from downtown. They were heading to the boy's place—a house he shared with others of his kind. The neighborhood was a maze of burned-out cars, discarded sofas, refrigerators, and trash. There were also children's toys—stuffed animals, some partially dismembered, thrown about the street. The few small children the Outsider had seen looked feral—not playtime children and he wondered if the plush toys were traps to weed out the weak.

The wild boy's place was no different than the rest—a single story that might once have been yellow, nondescript, inner-city tract house; a used-to-be lawn, chain-link fence, and a wheel-less truck on blocks in the drive. There was a large dog chained up to a tree in the yard—vicious, snarling and growling at the pair. The boy silenced it with a well-aimed kick as he walked up the cracked sidewalk to the house. The Outsider looped along behind—he was moving a bit differently now—lower, more saunter, less stroll. He followed the boy up to the porch and stood quietly as the boy pounded on the door. The Outsider reached over his head to a wooded crossbeam and pulled himself slightly up off the rough rotten boards and, without disdain, he took in the broken windows, rusted chairs and torn yellow-white pull-down shades—cheap circus decor.

The boy knocked six times—three, and then three again, in quick succession—not a police knock, but one that let whomever was listening know he was friendly and there. The door was cracked open from inside and the boy had to push his way into the darkness. The Outsider put his hand on the small of the boy's back and cautiously followed him through.

The inside of the house was dark and warm. There was a musty odor of wet fur and urine—it was not a place the Outsider would have normally felt comfortable in, and yet, he was glad to be there. The scent was not unpleasing to whom he was now becoming—a new man. There were five large males in the living room—great beasts in various stages of undress and agitation, prowling, then lounging, stabs of dark, well-hung, energy flashing, coming to rest—they looked hungry, and there was an uneasiness just beneath the calm. There was nothing on the walls, and the furniture—or what passed for furniture—dirty sofas seemingly dragged from the street into the house, looked burrowed in, nested on. There were no chairs. The Outsider hung behind the boy, a bit to one side, waiting for an introduction that had yet to come.

"Fucking hit the liquor store on 53rd. You'd think that old chink would think better 'bout trying to stop it." The boy showed his cut hand—yapping loudly as he walked into the room. "Fuckin' old Mr. Chang, or Lee, or whatever the hell, got his melon popped. We hit Felix, too. Fucking dusted him man—that fat fuck is lying headless in a mother-fuckin' alley." The boy was a speedball of words—excited, filled with his day. He poured the story out like hot jet smoke into the room.

One of the males rose from his place on the sofa, and without acknowledging the Outsider, came toward the pair. He was nodding his head with a yes-yes move, and as he did so, he extended a hairy, muscled arm—palm up—for payment.

"Let's get it." Slow, guttural, a voice well suited for whisper torture threats. "Get what?" the boy asked. "The fucking money." The male sternly replied, "Come on, let's get it."

The boy started to explain, "It was shit, nothing at all, we got some gas and…" The room ignited—the uneasy calm bursting into an animal flash fire, flipping sofas, and sending any still air scrambling for the safety of the walls.

The large male grabbed the boy by the throat and forced him to the ground, quickly pinning him—he was fast for his size, but the Outsider, hanging back against the door, recklessly intervened, jumping over and then attacking the boy's assailant. The Outsider grabbed the large male by his hair and yanked the head back, savagely but not fatally, cracking the neck. The boy broke loose, scurried to a corner of the room and cowered against the wall, panting and waiting. The Outsider was almost full-sized now—the largest male there—and he could feel the strength flowing into his hands, bone hardening like quick steel on the forge. He owned this aggressive male and made no qualms about it. The Outsider dug his middle finger into the right eye of his catch, pushing into the head—clawing at the soft gelatinous orb. The large male howled with pain. The Outsider had not mentally debated his attack; he moved, instinct coursing through his blood—no hate, no anger, he had answered violence with violence, as all good beasts should. The other males half-circled, but unable to get purchase behind the Outsider, and unsure of this new threat, they did not attack. They stepped in, then out, a strange vicious dance of come and go—prodding the space in front of the battling pair. Teeth were flashed; yells and groans rent the air. The men jumped and shook their arms at him, but the Outsider held his place—knee against the large male's spine, strong hand wrapped in hair. Head pulled back, neck close to breaking, eye crushing with intent; the large male lay

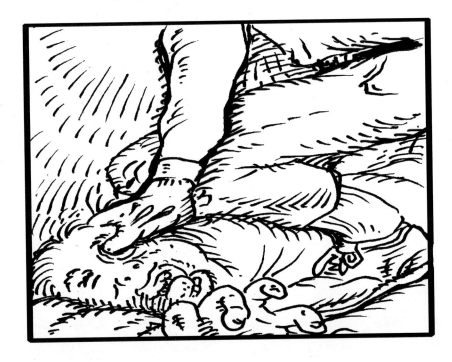

still beneath the Outsider—hurt, sobbing. The room slowly forced itself into a very uneasy stillness. The only sound now was the low heavy-air pumping of the man-beast's lungs. The boy crawled from the corner, stood and eased his way between the Outsider and the others. He bowed slightly and held his arm out, palm down as he addressed his man. "It's okay," his voice calm and relaxed. "He didn't mean anything. He's all right. Let him up, huh?"

The Outsider watched the boy's mouth without aggression, but he didn't quit, he dug his finger deeper into the eye. The boy now faced the others, pleaded one side to the next. "I met him downtown. He's okay, not us, but soon, eh—and good, huh, look at him, real good."

The group listened, but did not move. He turned back to the Outsider. "I'm all right, it's okay, man. You can let him loose huh? He's just him, yeah?" The boy was urgent but hopeful—it worked. The Outsider, calm but wary, released the man, who, now trying to be unseen, skulked to the back of the room. He initiated no eye contact with the other males, head down, unvoiced, but regulated by the others to a lesser place. The Outsider stood as erect as he could, and then he reached into his pocket and held out the gold tooth as an offering to the group.

"See!" the Boy exclaimed. "Fuckin' Felix, man, I told you, we did Felix."

The other males now showed their pleasure to the boy and the Outsider. They admired the tooth, passing it about, making simple hollows of their hands and rattle shaking the golden prize.

"This is good man, real good," the shorter, heavyset male who said this, reached over and stroked the boy with the back of his hand. He turned toward the Outsider, who now stood proudly before the group. "You got a name man?" the heavyset male asked. The Outsider thought for some time—a question like this should have been an easy answer, but he was unsure of his identity, unsure of whom he now was.

"Ha-ha!" the heavy male exclaimed. "This motherfucker is *No One*!" They all laughed, great deep rolling sounds of delight. The room filled with lunacy, animals braying at a handler's joke.

"Hey, you guys," the male continued, "No One, just gouged out T's eye! Hey T, did your eye just get out by itself?" The large wounded male, sitting against the wall briefly looked up and sheepishly displayed a cracked blood smile at the attention, but he remained in his place—at the back, as was now proper.

"Hey, T," one of the other males now joined in the calls. "You think No one wants to fuck your girl? You think he wants that?" The group, excited by the prospect of this, yelled and raged, but T did not join in—he neither looked up nor smiled.

The short, heavyset male quick shuffled into an adjoining room and came out with a female. She glanced quickly at the beaten T, which the Outsider assumed was her previous mate, before she was roughly dragged before him. She was naked, and the heavyset male pushed her down to the floor.

The girl went on hands and knees. The Outsider could see dark, angry bruises lying under a thick layer of dirt on her legs—likewise on her arms. Her hair was knotted at best, dirty blonde—real dirty blonde—and hanging almost to the floor. Her cunt was wet, more than excited—she'd been used, probably by T.

"Do you want that?" The heavyset male asked the Outsider. "Do you want to fuck that?" The Outsider looked the female over, but his cock had already made up its mind. The Outsider was harder than he'd been in years and rather than being put off by the dirt and the scent of her used cunt, he wanted her.

"Here," the big man gestured to the floor. "Fuck her here."

The Outsider pulled off his pants and crouched behind the female. His feet planted on the floor—spread legged squat— hands roughly holding her hips. The other men stood close by, watching him, murmuring grunts of approval and encouragement. The heavyset male yelled at her, "Back your ass up!"

She pushed back toward the Outsider—open, easy, no complaint or hesitation. She was his to do with as he would.

This wasn't love or any of the bullshit that Sheila had put him through. There was no god, no virginal missionary cunt, demanding the way a man might take a woman. This was as it should be, the body separated from the morals and attitudes of the weak. This was not abuse, rape, nor humiliation. The Outsider was a man and he would lay his seed in this woman. And she, feeling the strength of his worth, selfishly pushed against him and filled herself with the survival of her species— she surrendered her flesh to a man who could protect her young.

The Outsider threw hard, owning thrusts into the female and

when he came, he grew. One of the men grabbed the female by her hair and turned her face toward the Outsider. Her eyes rolled back into her head, her mouth hung open, her mind entranced with lust. Seeing the bitch's face, he knew himself now, and the years of his oppression poured from him as he came. He was no longer that powder-assed pussy, nancying about in his cheap car and life; he was as he always should have been—at his primal best—before he had been tamed. The Outsider leaned forward pushing the female beneath him and as she collapsed he sunk his teeth into her shoulder—biting through skin and muscle, to bone. In that way, he marked her, branded his new mate, and then he lifted his face from her flesh and raged bloody mouthed around the room—challenging the other males, but they let him reign. The Outsider stood on all fours now—naked, cum hanging from his cock, blood trickling from his mouth. The Outsider snarled at the men and then wickedly turned on the wild boy. He leapt and with his teeth grabbed the young male and tore his throat open. The Outsider wanted no memory of his weaker self, no ties to his old life. The Outsider gnawed at the boy's face, and with his new mouth he tore flesh from bone. He ripped at the boy's clothes and then, after tearing away his pants, the Outsider tore at the boy's cock, pulling the testicles from the body and holding them aloft. The other males jumped and danced at the edges of the room, the female whimpering, terrified, curled at her new mate's feet.

"I am not your man!" the Outsider roared, screaming at the boy's genitals. "*I* am not *your* man!"

It was then that he remembered the other female—the woman, Sheila, the one he'd been mated to, and the weak cubs that he had spawned. They could not be allowed to live. There was a male, too, a grocery clerk who had challenged his rule and needed to be dealt with. The Outsider swung toward the door aiming to set things right; and now, he ran down the street on all fours—naked and untamed.

An Honest Man

He was to be her fifth man that night, and the last one had been rough. Normally she could've seen it coming, but he took her unawares—flipped her, covered her mouth, and drove for her ass—entering deep and hard, before she could dislodge him with a sharp-toothed bite to his hand. She'd taken quite a beating for that one, but she recovered quickly, and it was still early. She averaged fifteen to twenty men a night—most of them pigs, with the occasional old goat thrown in to break the monotony of the contracted rape. But she was beautiful, long dark hair running like a night river down her back. Strong, olive-gold arms and legs, and her eyes were like a sunburst fire sinking into an Arabian sea—if you were looking for a whore, you couldn't do much better.

She painfully rose to her feet and staggered to a small corner washtub and cleaned her self. She spread her legs, and washed the remaining cum from between them. Sometimes she left it, and those who took her never cared. How many, she wondered, how many men had she gone through—had gone through her. And each time she'd coyly showed them the tattoo of the lantern stitched on her stomach, its golden glow searching for an honest man in a hostile world, and not one of them had recognized it for what it was. And there had been no gentle hands. She had the lantern placed there when she was thirteen, and the light from its colored-ink rays shimmered when she danced. The

tattoo went against what the religionists said about the body—
the temple of the Gods but, then again, what didn't? How many
believers had defiled her, used her, and disregarded their truth
for a few moments of lustful pleasure. She washed her arms and
then reached between her legs and gently patted the unclean
water against her bottom. There was blood on her hands, and
she hurt—badly.

A knock broke silence on the parlor door. "Cynthia? Cynthia?" The house mother was urgently calling her. She was ready. She put on a short silk gown, perfumed her neck and her inner thighs, and then she went to look for him. Rather, she became ready to see if this next one might be an honest man.

****

The first time she was taken, she was eight years old. It was an uncle, a kindly old man she'd always adored. They were not related by blood, but Uncle was what he was called.

He came to her home on the outskirts of the city and her father, mother and three brothers welcomed him—she was happy to see him. She ran and threw her arms about his neck when he arrived. He had always been kinder to her than either her mother or father was. They did not show the affection that this man gave her. There was a dinner that day—a feast of sorts—and she sat near Uncle, his hand gently on her leg, or softly touching the back of her hair. He was always so kind.

After dinner her mother informed her that she was to go with him, to stay with Uncle in his home. And, contrary to what you might think a child would do, Cynthia was happy to leave. Her brothers had never been kind. They were foul, angry boys, who'd been taught by her father to steal and con. They hustled the streets near the city-center, robbing tourists and pulling quick-money scams. Her father, when he was home and looked at her, saw her not as a daughter, but as something the family could profit from. At first she thought his glances were looks of pride and love but then, as she got older, she realized that he looked at her as one might look at coins found in the street—a prize to be taken and spent. And her mother... frankly, even at eight years old, she wasn't sure who her mother was. Yes, this woman lived here, but besides being a cook, a maid, and a whore to her father, her mother was no one. She might as well have called the chair she sat in "mother"—it cradled her, and the chair put its arms about her when she climbed into its lap.

She drove off with Uncle, happy.

His house was to her, a palace—a great villa that stood on a hill overlooking the place where she'd lived. There were many rooms in Uncle's home, each one larger and grander than the last, and he had a bath—a large, ornately tiled tub that he filled with water; hot, clean water. She'd usually bathed with her mother in the river, and while she enjoyed the flow, it was cold at times, and dirty. Uncle was kind. When it was time to bathe, he removed her old clothes and gently placed her in the tub. The water felt good against her body, the soft waves of the currents gently caressing her. Uncle removed his things and climbed in. She had seen naked men before, but she laughed at his large hairy body. "You're like a bear, Uncle!" she giggled, "A great big bear."

Uncle smiled and took soap into his hands. He reached out for her arms and he lovingly cleansed her young skin. She closed her eyes and smiled, he was so much gentler than her mother, who, when bathing her handled her roughly. Uncle had her stand in the tub and he covered her body with soap—it was wonderful. When Uncle finished he stepped out and held a large pink towel for her. It was so different than the rough wool sheets of her family—this towel was soft as a summer field flower, as a cloud might feel. He dried her and then he put sweet powder on his hands and ran them across her flesh. Uncle then picked her up, and carried her to his room. It was a room larger than she'd ever been in, with tapestries on the wall and a great round bed in the center. The windows—archways to the street—were open and the curtains gently swayed with the warm desert breeze. She had never been happier.

Uncle laid her on the bed, leaned over, and gently kissed her stomach. She leaned back and relaxed—the way things are now she thought—how wonderful to be here. Uncle, still naked, climbed over her body, straddled her young form and continued his kissing—soft butterflies dancing across her neck and cheeks. He spread her legs now and leaned down below her stomach. He kissed her again, this time wetter, more mouth than kiss. And it felt strange. She thought she might wet the bed, and wouldn't Uncle be mad then, but she didn't, and then he kissed his way back up her stomach towards her face, and again her smile lit his way. He held her hands outstretched and spread her legs wider than before—with his legs inside—gently, but firmly bracing them open. And then, as his kind face came all the way up to hers, she felt something hard where he'd kissed—something pushing against her lower stomach—making her uncomfortable. She wiggled against it, tried to move away, but Uncle held her and his face now came down over hers. The hard thing pushed against her. Up into her stomach and she struggled. Uncle held her down.

"You're hurting me," she said. But Uncle didn't stop.

He covered her mouth with his, forcing his tongue inside, causing her to swallow. He tasted sour and she couldn't breathe. The pain between her legs was greater now and tears ran from her eyes as if to get away. She tried with all her strength to get up, but if she rose and came toward him, the pain in her stomach got deeper, further in, hurt more.

"No Uncle!" She cried and shook her face loose. "Please! No Uncle, NO!"

But it was as if Uncle was sleeping, he wouldn't hear her, and he didn't stop. Cynthia hurt, she hurt all over. He pressed down deeper into her and when he pulled away she bit her lip *hard*, transferring the pain to her mouth, somehow controlling the hurt. Now she did wet herself, a warm release down her legs and thighs. Uncle wrestled with her a bit more before he put his whole weight down upon her—a weight so great that it swallowed Cynthia—and then he rested. She was glad it stopped, and slowly the thing that had invaded her softened and went away.

She was there nearly two years, and after a while she got used to being used. She never saw her family, and rarely left the house. A week after her 10th birthday, Uncle went to the store and never returned. Men came a few days later and took her, gave her to the house that she now lives in—gave her a new mother, and new uncles.

****

There was a doctor coming that morning. Someone from the city had complained about the condition of the house. In response, the rooms were swept; the beds were made, and good food was brought in. It was not the house that she knew, but it made no difference—if things were nice, they were never nice long.

When it was her turn to be examined, she was taken to one of the larger rooms. There was a doctor there, and a woman in white, writing on a tablet. The doctor was kind; he spoke with her a while—pleasant talk to make her feel at ease, but there was no need, she was going to do whatever they wanted. The doctor asked her to disrobe and then he turned his back to talk with the woman. Cynthia took off everything and stood unashamed, her bruised and beaten body exposed. When the doctor turned back around he was flustered. "No, no, dear," he said. "Here, put this on." The woman in white helped her. Cynthia stepped into a strange gown with ties in the back—a white, soft cotton dress with petite printed flowers sprinkled over the cloth. The doctor asked for her arm and gently pushed back the sleeve of her gown. He ran his hand so tenderly over her bruises, a look of concern on his face. "How did you get these, dear?" he asked "Do they hit you?"

Cynthia looked up into his eyes, preparing to give the story she was taught by the house mother, that she had fallen, was the clumsy sort, should've known better, but then, on meeting his glance she recoiled. For there, burning deep inside his eyes was a light, not unlike the glow from her lantern, but brighter, stronger, *real*. It was kindness and love, and it momentarily flickered before it was lost with a blink. She immediately reached down and attempted to lift her gown. He stopped her hands.

"No, please," he said. But then she tried again. "Are you trying to show me something?" he asked. Cynthia nodded her head yes, and as he let her, she pulled up her gown. She showed the doctor the image of the lantern tattooed onto her stomach—the golden glow searching for an honest man and she looked at him with hope in her eyes.

"It's very beautiful." he said. "Is that what you wanted to show me?"

"Yes," she softly spoke, "I thought you would know."

The doctor smiled and asked when she'd gotten it. "A man came here a while ago. He spoke in the square outside, and after he talked to the gathered crowd he sat and told me a story of love and kindness. He said that somewhere there was an honest man, and if I searched for him, he could be found. After he left, I got the lantern inked into my flesh, so I could remember his story and maybe one day an honest man would see it, and know."

The doctor lowered her gown as he smiled at Cynthia. He was kind, and as before, gentle. "We're going to check your blood," he told her. "Are you okay with that?" Cynthia held out her wrist. "No," the doctor laughed slightly. "Here, sit down." He held her arm. "A slight stick, here." He touched the crook of her elbow. "It'll be quick, I promise. And then a shot—vitamins, for your health."

The woman in white drew the blood and Cynthia kept her eyes on the doctor. It was him, she knew it. He was gentle and kind. He cared for her. When the woman withdrew the needle and the small cotton-puffed bandage had been put in its place, the doctor turned to leave. Cynthia reached for him, tenderly held his arm to entreat him to stay. But he removed her hand, smiled and assured her that one day he would return. Here at last was her success. Thousands of men, cities of foul intentioned *johns* had passed through her, but now she had found him—and she knew, like his word, that he would return—and she could wait.

****

"Cynthia? Cynthia?" the house mother was calling her. She was ready. She put on a short silk gown, perfumed her neck and her inner thighs and then laid waiting on the bed.

The door opened and there he was, but without his doctor's coat, and without nurse or bag. He had come for her. She arose from the bed and held out her arms. He stepped inside, wrapped himself in her and gently kissed her lips. She responded in kind, so gentle, so perfect—so honest. He removed her silk gown and she stepped out, as if stepping into the gardens of heaven. He gently laid her down on the bed—a bed that before had been a platform of pain—a rack built to torture her most tender soul, but now that bed was an altar of truth. He held her hands out to the side, and with his knees, he spread her legs. She knew what to do and she pushed her hips toward him, accepting his love, seeking the spark in his eyes so she could be consumed by the fire that he bore, and he filled her. He let her arms go and she wrapped them around him, she squeezed and danced beneath him—a thousand men to get to this one—a thousand nights of despair to find one honest man in a world that was populated by vanity, lust, and hurt. She brought him closer than any person had ever been to her, and now she could feel his urgency—his body so near to hers, she felt him shake, release, and then go still. The room was filled by the silence of hope.

"Fuck..." he cursed. "I knew you'd be great."

"And I knew you were him," she said, "I knew you had to be him."

The doctor stood up and quickly grabbed his pants. "What?" He asked. Cynthia sat up on the bed. "An honest man," she said, "I knew you were an honest man."

"Ha!" the doctor laughed, "Yes, I guess I am, and great you were." He threw a handful of crumpled dollars at her. "Here you go, baby."

He walked out.

****

The city was a swarm of dirt that hung in the air—the dust kicked up from the street was so foul that it refused to lie back upon itself; it clung to the children and the beggars in the square. Cynthia stoically walked through the crowd while whispers of *whore* shadowed her steps. She was looking for him, the man who spoke of honesty and love, but if he wasn't there, she knew there would be others—puppets of an unseen god, chanting and casting a message of white-light hope before a gullible crowd. And they were there, these men, some of whom had fucked her, beaten her—all had lied to her. They stood together, clustered on a stage. One of them, his long white robes raised high above the filth, spoke his piece…

"And behold, I say to you."

Cynthia screamed above the crowd. "There is no God here!" She cried, "Look at me," she yanked up her dress exposing herself to the throng. "You're liars. He does not exist!"

The crowd erupted in screams. They clawed at her, beat her with their fists, and she let them. She took their fury and their hate; she consecrated herself in the true kindness of these beasts and then she fell to the ground, unconscious, and was nearly trampled to death by the crowd.

When Cynthia awoke, she was face down in the dirt and she could taste the city filth mingled with the blood in her mouth. She was being licked. A dog, a mangy street cur, was tenderly ministering to her wounds. She sat up, involuntarily wet herself, and then reached out to the cur. The dog, although a stray, didn't run from her touch, it pulled near—gave itself to her. It was the only true affection Cynthia had ever received.

"Why aren't we this?" she said, looking into the dog's eyes. "We talk so," she gestured to the holy men still preaching, the hems of their robes flecked by her blood. "But in all we've done, we can't show the kindness or the honor that these street curs show each other. And, even with nothing, they behave so far above we who pray, who recognize a God. What good is that anyway, to recognize something that we can't attain? Better to recognize this street," she reached down and held the dirt in her hands, "better to recognize the mud of the city, the clinging filth of our days, because this," she held the dirt aloft, "this is what

we *can* subscribe to—this is what we can be. This is a goal already met by our kind." She slowly rose and limped back towards the brothel, rubbing the soil of the city through her hair. "This," she said, "this, is what we are."

Deconstructing God

Job was having a hard time getting the blowtorch to light. It looked easy on the directions, but he wasn't very mechanically inclined. He wasn't exactly sure how to use it either, especially for the purpose he intended, but it wasn't like he could fuck it up—burned skin, after all, was burned skin, whether or not you knew how to burn it—now, if he could just get it lit.

The man in the chair was starting to come around, but Job wasn't ready for him yet, so he took the incense infused rag and covered the man's nose and mouth—a couple quick breaths, and he was under again. It hadn't been easy to catch him—it took years actually, and it ate up the last of Job's money, but he got him. The funny thing was, after chasing this prick all over the world—and he left a trail as wide as the Amazon—Job caught him when he realized that he was already there, and he'd stopped looking.

Self-realization can be a funny thing. Psychiatrists have talked for years about people having "white light" experiences, or "God flashes"—a shift in thinking, attitude, or ideas, that seemingly comes from outside one's self. It's all very nice, but when *you* get one—that brilliant thought that supposedly came directly from the Almighty, well, it really can be quite miraculous, and, in this case, a touch ironic. Job used a "God thought" to kidnap God and, for once, the Big Honcho in the

Sky was the instrument of his own undoing, instead of him being the architect of so many others' pain.

Job slapped the passed-out body—a violent ringing shot that jerked the man's face hard to the right—and a wave tore through the world. The ground shook, reverberating from the slap to the end of existence, but Job didn't care; he had him now. He had caught God, and the blowtorch sprang to life.

****

It was on a Monday, a workday, a pray about not losing your job day. Job had placed himself directly in front of the tallest building of finance—a building dedicated to the "in God we trust" side of this Man. Where better, if God were going to be anywhere, than this building? God had always wanted to be served and adored. Job dressed himself in the clothes of a street beggar, a modern-day leper on 2nd Street, a one-hand-out pain in the ass creeping desperately along the boulevard. God could never resist a beggar; especially if it looked like that beggar's skin was in danger of peeling away. Job had recently become a very cunning man. He wasn't always so, but circumstances had forced him to evolve. The day before, he had stopped by a butcher's shop and picked up a bucket of lamb's blood—fresh, un-coagulated Little Bo Peep purity—and he had bathed himself in it that morning. In his pocket was a rag infused with dust of Myrrh.

He knew it was going to be hard to spot him. It wasn't like God would roll up all bearded and robed, voice thundering throughout the city. God was a tricky fuck; he could be anyone. But Job had a feeling that it would be something in the eyes and general behavior of the man, woman, or child, he'd make contact with—something beyond worldly that would give God away. Job sat at the curb for hours before God showed, and it wasn't too surprising that when he did come, God was in the guise of a stock trader—a business type, a briefcase-slinging-gunfighter of commerce. He walked up real close to Job, close enough to smell him. He had his wallet out, ready to contribute, and he hadn't even been asked yet. It was the lamb's blood, chum on the skin of man that drew in the Great Holy Shark of the universe.

"Here you go buddy," the man who just might be God said as he handed Job a dollar bill, "a little something to make it easier. You have a good day now, okay?" *Oh, wasn't he the benevolent one,* Job thought. The man had a kind face, but not soft—a strong jawline and a male-model nose. He also had light brown hair with just a touch of distinguished grey at the temples. The man who might be God was as handsome and perfect as a poster boy for stock traders, and then, Job looked into his eyes; or rather, he looked through his eyes and was sucked into a telescope of light as deep as the cosmos. Thank this man before him that Job had covered himself with lamb's blood, or he would've most surely been caught, and his unrighteous intentions displayed before the most Holy of Hosts. God was thankfully distracted by the scent of the blood—and Job's intent of malice went unseen.

'Thank you, sir." Job was quick with the pleasantries. "But it already is going to be a great day."

"And why's that, son?" He who was now most assuredly God asked.

"Because, I'm going to see something that I've never seen before, something, even greater than *this*.' Job reverently held up the dollar bill. The man before him, or rather his eyes, the same as the one drawn over the great pyramid, looked at the money and with a touch of self-absorbed interest questioned Job again.

"And what could that possibly be?" God asked.

"I'm going to see a sacrifice," Job replied, "a real burnt offering."

The man who would be God perked up—he'd just gotten an inside line on an under-the-table trade. "Really," he asked, "and can just anyone see this…uh…offering?"

Job had him, and now he needed to reel him in, and out of public view. There was a van waiting at the rear of the building, tucked into the loading dock.

"I don't know," Job carefully displayed his thoughts. "I guess so.

Hell, why not? I've got a vehicle parked out back... that is, if you'd like to come?' God looked Job over, judging him on his not-exactly-homeless ruse, but Job caught it.

"I know,' Job said, gesturing to his circumstance, "It ain't really honest, but a guy has to make a living, right?"

The man, the one called God, smiled. "Yeah, I guess you're right. Now let's go take a peek at that offering."

They walked toward the rear of the building, God on occasion deeply inhaling, filling himself with the scent of the blood beneath Job's clothes. It was like a plateful of hot cookies to a hungry child, a room chock-full of grandma's house aroma— and Job led this living, most dangerous Creator out behind the building.

The van was rented. It was a cargo type, black with tinted windows. If you were of the paranoid sort, you might think it a vehicle to transport agents of the government, but it wasn't. Job had picked it up from Harold's on W. 30th, a cut-rate rental place that wasn't too particular when it came to the moral or dirty-business leanings of their renters.

"The door can be a bit sticky," Job warned God. "Here," he reached out and opened it for Him. "You get what you pay for, huh?"

God began to climb in, but just when he got up on the seat, Job pulled the Myrrh-infused rag from his pocket, reached around

and covered God's nose and mouth with it. The deity dropped like a swarm of drunken locusts on Egypt, and Job quickly shoved his Most Holy Ass into the back of the van. He then took duct tape and secured the rag to God's face, and with a couple of solid wraparounds, they were off. Quick and smooth as a whistle, God was luggage—no one else had seen it.

It was a ballsy move, this God trap that Job had sprung, and he'd been guessing really; would the lamb's blood lull God into a satiated state of docileness? Would the Myrrh really knock him out? Job wasn't sure, and he was risking an eternity in Hell on his guesses. But Job was very angry at the passed out Creator lying in the cargo area of his van. So, whether it worked or not, he'd been willing to try. What was that old Bible line, *"...if you have faith and do not doubt, not only can you do what was done to the fig tree, but also you can say to this mountain, 'Go, throw yourself into the sea,' and it will be done,"* Job had faith.

Job had grown up listening to the trouble that this Man had caused—the death, the destruction, the wars, and the natural disasters that have shaken this world since its creation, they'd all originated from this man, this duct-taped, cargo-riding fuck. And Job had also tasted a bit of God's handiwork himself, and it was that taste that brought him to this place.

Job drove the van out to a block of old warehouses near the docks. He was neither stopped nor questioned along the way— with God out of the picture, things were running very smoothly in the world. He pulled in front of one of the smaller buildings, hopped out, and rolled up the big double door of the warehouse. He drove the van in and pulled the door down behind him. Job had the room prepared, he'd sprinkled lamb's blood on the floor, and now he hurriedly lit the incense that he'd placed in large burners at each corner of the room—sweet, spicy, smoke began to rise. Smoke to keep the big mean God sedated and unable to reach into his bag of Godly tricks. *Job was gonna let him have it.* God would soon be held accountable for his crimes against humanity. The Heavenly Cargo was dragged from the van and rough-rope tied to a chair—*now, where was that fucking torch?*

****

Job ran the flame close to God's face and it left a Haley's Comet trail of burnt flesh. "Wakey, wakey, Mr. God. It's time to meet your Makey." Job had been desperately waiting for this moment, and he was a bit giddy—a lot giddy, borderline manic actually. "WAKE UP, MOTHERFUCKER!" Job screamed as he punched God in the balls.

"What, what are you doing?" God asked, at first groggy and then more insistent. "Where am I? *What are you doing?*"

"You don't know?" Job was happier than he'd been in years. "The big Map-Maker in the Sky doesn't know where he is? I thought you created *all* this?" Job twirled around the room like a demented Julie Andrews. "We're in that piece of shit warehouse that you built on the waterfront—the one near your homeless camp, off 24th."

"What are you talking about? I didn't build anything. What are you doing?" God was slowly coming around.

"I'm getting ready for an offering—one that you wanted to see, a big chunk of your Holy flesh in exchange for all the innocents you've killed."

"I didn't kill anybody. I'm a stock trader for fuck sake. Let me go!"

The air was thick with incense—not enough to put God under, but a floating cloud of heavenly local anesthesia drifting through the air. Job walked over to a table and picked up a pair of bolt cutters—a short, red handled pair—mostly made to be breaking bike locks, and he waved them at God before sauntering back toward him. Job rolled up a desk chair and sat before his Creator. He was burning-bush close.

"You ever see someone lose a hand, or a finger?" Job asked. "Oh, wait, what am I saying, of course you have. You've seen lots of that, yeah? It's a shame, because you did such a beautiful job making these." Job reached out and stroked God's hand. God tried to move it, pull away, but his arms were anchored to the chair, his wrists securely tied down. Job caressed God's ring finger—a gold band—knowing it was about to be lopped off and rolling on the floor.

"Stop it!" The Man screamed. "I don't know you, I didn't do anything! I'm not who you think I am."

Job fumed in anger. "YOU DIDN'T DO ANYTHING?" He stood and leaned over God, shouting in his face. "YOU DIDN'T FUCKING DO ANYTHING? You're not who I think you are? I know who you are motherfucker, and I have a beginning-of-the-world list of your crimes. How many fucking people have you killed?"

Job took the bolt cutters and chopped off the ring finger of God—the bone breaking as easily as a brittle winter branch—and as the finger fell it disintegrated in mid air, a clean cut and break, and there was no blood.

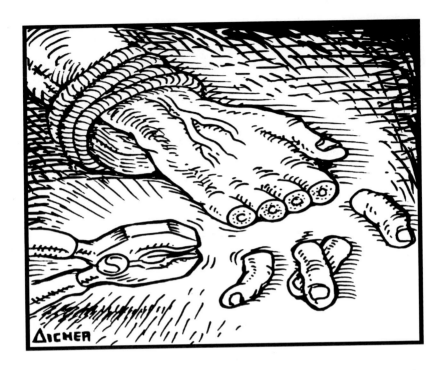

"Well, look at that," Job proudly exclaimed. "Disappearing fingers, and no blood—and you said I didn't know who you were. Well, fuck you. I know you. Does it hurt? Can you even feel pain?"

God gave Job the look of one resigned to his fate, but it wasn't a completely resigned look. There *was* anger there—a stern hurricane stare that tore through the smoke-filled room like lightning through a black snowstorm. The world shook, and the coasts of Africa became none.

"I don't care if you can feel it," Job told God, "because I can. I can feel good about this, and what I'm going to do to you. I'm gonna take you down one pride-filled piece at a time—so many crimes you'll pay for, so many lives." Job reached down, pulled up his trousers, and grabbed a large knife that he had strapped to his leg. He brandished it, flashed it through the air, and sliced God's face, not once, but many times, each cut punctuated with a word—

"One."

"Fucking."

"Piece."

"Atta."

"Time."

Job stopped slicing and snatched a roll of parchment from the table—it was a large roll, 10 or 12 inches across—and as he displayed it, God could see written across the top, in a hand steady and true: "Crimes Committed Against the World by His Most Unholy Lord – actual name and address unknown." Job read the first charge:

The person known as God was seen killing two innocent lambs in order to clothe a creation, Man, which he had made. The lambs were given no chance to defend themselves—they were skinned, brutally.

"Ha!" Job exclaimed. "The first in what looks to be a very long day of atonement. Innocent lambs—animal abuse is a crime worthy of at least this." Job took the torch to God's right ear and watched intently as it melted in the flame like a wax candy treat. God grimaced but did not scream and the continent of Asia also melted into nothingness.

Job worked well into the evening slashing and burning his way into the 21st century. The list of crimes levied against God was horrible and frightening, and Job carried out his punishments with zeal. Job spoke for those who could not. He struck back for those who had been hit, and he burned flesh for the holocaust of the ages. God, still tied to the chair, was less than he had been—his toes and fingers gone, his clothes burnt from his body and his flesh seared to bone, but he was still conscious, and the world had become an island, of only this room, and these two—Job and God.

The scroll had been unrolled—a mile of parchment—laying brown paper spent, covering the floor of the room in large, damning piles.

"And now it's my turn," Job said. He reached into his breast pocket and pulled out a small photo of a woman—brunette, kind face, tender love-touched eyes and lips—a worn cherished photo.

"Do you remember her?" Job asked God. "Do you remember this one?"

Job grabbed the back of God's head, his fingers sinking into the now putrid flesh, and he pulled him close. He held the photo before what used to be God's eyes.

"Look at her!" Job ordered God. "Do you remember her? This was my wife, and you took her."

God shook his head no.

Job screamed, "Don't fucking *no* me! Look at her!" He shoved the photo into God's face.

"She was an angel! A fucking angel and she never hurt anyone. You had no right to take her. You had no fucking right!" Job slapped God as hard as he could, spit slow-motion flying from the deity's mouth. "What had she done to you, to anyone? I loved her! What the fuck had I done to you for you to take her from me?"

"Say something!" Job screamed and gestured to the world that was no longer around them. He waved at the emptiness of retribution. "Fucking, say something! You did this! You fucking caused this!"

God whispered low on his breath, the words falling from his mouth as a beaten dove falls from the sky.

"What did you say?" Job asked almost as quietly—intense, listening for some remorse. "What did you just say?"

God's eyes were gone, his nose broken, his teeth swallowed into the stomach of his pain.

"Speak!" Job ordered. "Say something!"

"You can't do this," God said. "You can't do this, Job."

"But I can do it," Job said, "and I did. I made you pay for what you've done. I'm holding you accountable."

God looked in the direction of his accuser—he was incapable of seeing him, but he knew where he was.

"You can't kill me Job, because this is *my* dream. I dreamed you, and the heavens, and the earth, I created all this as I slept. *You* can't kill *me*."

They were both silent now, the still of an eternal night wrapped itself around what was left of the universe and then Job moved closer, smiled and said, "but I can do it. I believe I can, I have faith, and it's your promise, and for her, I will."

As Job plunged the knife into the heart of God, the lights went out in the world.

The Crosstown Bulls: A Love Story

Richard cowered behind the small chain-link fence. He was in danger of getting beaten, stomped to death, actually, by the large bull dyke Margaret and her companion, Ida. The ladies were a pair of what the small men in the neighborhood called "Battle Dykes"—a couple of large, cruising thugs who would like nothing more than to have a bit of brutal sport with a gentle man like Richard. And Richard was also in a gang of sorts, or a protection society, a group of Nancy Boys who figured they'd better band together before they were ripped apart. Richard closed his eyes and held his breath. He was hoping for safe passage. No such luck.

"Well, look-it here…" One of the dykes grabbed Richard by the neck and hoisted him over the fence like a plucked flower shaking dirt from its stem.

"What you got, Margaret?" Her companion jumped in—and on.

"Looks like I got me a little *ass-cleaner* with a real sweet mouth. "She made Richard pucker by squeezing his cheeks—hard. "What do you say, 'little lady'?"

"I'm a man, dammit. You let me go!" Richard hung from her hand, kicking and squirming in the air. "Let me go!" he screamed. "Let me go!"

"Now, why would I do that?" Margaret asked sarcastically. "I'm feeling all gushy-wushy back there." She rubbed her large ass with her free hand, "and I need tending to."

"Why don't we take him 'round back?" Ida said, "I could use a 'lil sprucing up myself."

The big bulls laughed, took a quick look around, and then carried Richard to a place a touch more private on the shady side of the building.

"Come on Ida, pull his things off."

Margaret held Richard around the chest as Ida pulled off his shoes and pants—her large fingers were not gentle—ripping and tearing his fine garments. Richard had on a pair of light blue bikini briefs beneath his trousers, and these brought the two bulls no small measure of enjoyment, until the briefs were ripped off, and his extremely small penis was exposed.

"Well, fucking look at that!" Ida was pointing and laughing. She grabbed one of Richard's legs and held it high in the air, spread-eagling the poor half-naked man. She took a finger and put it aside his cock—her little finger, his even littler prick. She squealed with laughter. "Your buddies must have thimble asses!"

This was rough sport and it was about to get rougher.

Margaret threw Richard to the ground and flipped him onto his back. Ida held him as Margaret dropped her very large, very

94

dirty trousers and exposed her equally large and, extremely dirty ass. She sat squarely down on Richards face, burying his head between her quite ample bare ass-cheeks.

"Clean it up, bitch!" She wriggled, and sunk lower, covering the poor man.

Richard thrashed about on the ground trying to get a breath. He was in danger of suffocating—beginning to feel lightheaded—when Margaret shifted forward and let him catch a whiff of stale, sour air. He gasped.

"You either start licking little lady," she hissed, "or I take you out."

Richard knew that if he didn't follow orders, she would kill him, and being suffocated by a large, unclean woman's ass was not his way to go. He dutifully stuck out his tongue and tentatively licked a cheek. She shifted up again.

"You're going to get hurt bitch, if you don't get in that hole *right now*. Stop fucking around and clean it!" Margaret took her hands and spread her ass cheeks wide, exposing her anus. "Lick it!" she commanded.

This time Richard knew better than to fight, and he put his tongue against Margaret's hole and licked. It tasted sharp and sour at the same time, but like a good boy he did his job. Licking and cleaning the large woman's behind—he also found that the more he licked, the less it tasted, so like a dog, he hungrily lapped at her ass.

"That's it baby, lick it up," Margaret's deep gravelly voice cooed.

"Hey, we gotta a good one here," Ida moaned and rubbed her fat crotch. "We should take him back and, oh fuck!" Ida pointed toward Richard's genitals. "Look at that, look at his little dick!" Margaret looked down.

Richard was erect.

"Oh my god, Margaret. Your 'lil ass cleaner's dick is hard. Look out! He's gonna put your fucking eye out with that thing." The bulls mocked and roared with laughter.

Across the street, a small gang of Nancy Boys were getting their nerve up to intervene, and steeled by their feminine protective nature, they huddled together like a bevy of 15-year-old school girls and then smooth-hustled their way across the street.

"Hey you!" One of the Nancys yelled. "Stop it! Stop it right there."

One of the braver boys had picked up a small, broken tree branch and he was leading the charge. It was Tommy, a real keen dancer from Temple City.

The bulls looked up toward the Boys like a couple of lions

interrupted while tearing apart a half-eaten gazelle. They were more irritated by the soft invasion of their playtime than they were about the Cuban heel-clicking advance of the Boys. Undeterred, they turned back to their sport. There was another ass to clean. Richard wasn't done, and Ida took her turn.

The Nancy Boys moved closer—brave Tommy led again. He advanced on the pair and whacked at Ida's back with his branch—it broke. His palms stung from the force of the blow. Ida lifted her fat ass from Richard's face and shook Tommy like an extremely well put-together rag doll. A simple gold bracelet fell from his wrist, and his pocketbook skittered off under a bush.

"Eeeeeeeeeeeee!"

It was a high-pitched scream that, instead of frightening the other Nancys, inflamed them and they swarmed the big bulls— six Nancys on two battle dykes. They might as well have been beating on a rock. They did manage to dislodge Richard though, and after getting his breath, he scuttled to his feet and tried to run. But Margaret quickly grabbed him, tucked him under her arm, and jogged toward the back of the building. Ida followed.

They could have beaten these Boys if that was their whim, but instinctively they knew that a large commotion meant police presence, so they half-hurriedly made their way down the walk. The Boys chased, but to the Bulls, they were no more dangerous than an expensively perfumed cloud of agitated dust. The big dykes turned the corner and ran down the alley with their prey,

Richard, dangling beneath Margaret's large arm like a scuffed-up kid leather handbag.

****

The Bulls took Richard to a clubhouse bar on the far side of town—he knew where it was. Sometimes the Nancys, after getting liquored up, would drive by and yell curses at the windows—their light pink cosmopolitans coaxing brave threats from the boys. Richard never thought he would ever be inside. It smelled. The bar had that sour malt odor, and Richard wasn't exactly sure if it was the spilt beer on the floor or a contagion of yeast infections. He grimaced, smacked his lips and thought about the thick taste of Margaret's behind.

There were quite a few dykes inside, and catcalls and laughter danced drunkenly around Richard as he was pawed at and groped. They stripped off the rest of his clothes and forced him into a leather harness—a gay gladiator's suit with loops and studs. Richard's frail body struggled to fill it out, and it sagged very unfashionably on him. He was led by chain to a dark corner of the bar and forced to kneel on worn red carpet. Here he was secured; legs and arms behind him, head tied with a leather chord and pulled forcefully back, and he was chained to a metal bar—handcuffed, and not going anywhere. If Richard hadn't recently completed the Linda Fairchild Yoga Series it would have surely broken his neck.

Margaret was at the bar writing with thick black pen on a piece of cardboard. From Richard's now very limited viewpoint, it looked like a sign of some sort. She finished and walked over to him, holding the cardboard out for his perusal—it read: TOILET. She took a metal coat hanger and placed it around his neck—hung the sign from it. Richard was mortified. This was worse than he thought. The big bulls lined up one after the other, and they took turns letting their digested beer loose in Richard's face.

He gagged and sputtered on the urine, but it did him no good. Some of the dyke's streams were so hard and long that Richard was forced to inhale, choke and, unfortunately, swallow most of their waste. Thankfully, his tears didn't show on his piss-soaked face. Surely the Nancy Boys would rescue him soon, but after many, "Merle Haggard on the jukebox," hours of being a toilet, no one had showed. On the other side of town, the Nancy Boys

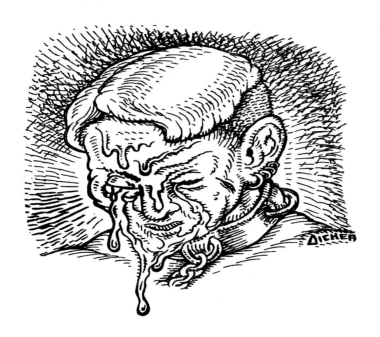

were putting together an almost brave plan—it involved a quick recon move. One of the Boys had peeped through the Bull's clubhouse windows and spotted their living porcelain receptacle friend, being abused by a large and dangerous group of women. The Nancy's plan was to don black garb—not leather mind you—more of a form-fitting, dark grey, chiffon, and then break into the bar and sneak Richard out after everyone had left. They also planned to procure a shit load of ballet slippers, preferably unworn, and the majority, a nice size seven men's.

****

It was a long night for Richard. His neck was sore and cramped from having his head pulled back. His throat burned from the urine and the acid of regurgitation, and his stomach was distended, filled with the piss of fifty beer-quaffing Bulls. He was sure he looked quite the mess.

The bar was empty now except for a few voices. Richard couldn't see who they belonged to but one of them was most definitely Margaret's. She was giving instructions to someone—someone with a gentler, more feminine voice—but not a man.

"You get the bitch hosed down and clean this place up," Margaret ordered. "Rodrigo will get the glasses in the morning, but I want the fucking floor swept and the bar wiped down. Ida and I are going up to bed, so you keep yourself and *her* quiet, and I want you to secure our little piss-pot in the back room and cover her with a towel. We don't want our toilet to go dying on

100

us…" A deep evil laugh punctuated that last order. Richard heard heavy retreating footsteps and a door slam. He was alone with the gentle voiced girl.

Richard could hear movement and then what sounded like a faucet being screwed on when suddenly he was hit with a cold-water spray. *He* was the *bitch* getting hosed down. The water stung and was uncomfortable, but Richard soon leaned into it as he caught the fresh-air scent that it brought. He retched, threw up nearly a quart of ingested piss, and then inhaled deeply of the clean, cold stream. He was hurting, but this impromptu bathing felt good, and after retching again, he felt sore but better—almost.

A face appeared over Richard's now. She looked young and not unkind—mid-20s, brunette, with easy doe brown eyes. *What was she doing hanging with this crowd? Maybe she was just coming up; the new girl on the scene.* Either way, she was a hell of a lot more put together than Ida or Margaret; Richard envied her fresh, clean skin.

"God, look what they've done to you." The girl pushed Richard's wet bangs away from his eyes. At first, he recoiled from her touch, but now he craved her soft hand. "You're a mess, baby." Richard started to sob as she unlocked the shackles on his feet, removed the chain.

"You better not run now,' she warned. She was kind, but firm and Richard shook his head *no*. He was scared and he hadn't the strength to run. The girl continued freeing Richard from his bonds and when she loosed the tie holding his head back, he stretched and then lowered his gaze—he was embarrassed, humiliated over the abuse that he'd taken. The girl walked to the bar, grabbed a clean towel, and then came back and wrapped it around Richard. She gently patted and rubbed him dry.

"Can I ask you something?" Richard's voice was weak, shaky, and apologetic. He waited for a reply.

"Sure," the girl said softly. "What do you want to know?"

"You're not like them. Why are you here? Why are you being kind to me?"

The girl laughed "I am like them, kind of, but I guess I'm just here for protection, really."

Richard thought on that a moment, and he was about to prod for her story, but then he realized that that was how he got involved with the Nancy Boys. He wasn't really like them, but he was small, picked on a lot, and women frightened him. He didn't hate girls; actually he kind of liked the way they looked. Not those big dykes, of course, but ones like this… this…

"What's your name?" he asked.

"They call me Bunny," the girl replied, "Little Bunny."

"That's nice," Richard said. "Real nice."

****

Outside, the Nancy Boys were ready to make their move. They'd arrived in three cars; two olive-green Subaru wagons with sport roof racks, and a long black Lincoln Town Car. *Richard was probably upset and they thought a touch of luxury might ease his pain.* They also had baseball bats—not heavy hitters, but little Louisville Sluggers, and they meant business. From the bushes across the street they'd watched the bar clear out, and now they figured it was safe to go in. They were going to rescue Richard—silent, cat-like, they tip toed toward the door.

****

Richard was sitting next to Bunny—she was patting him on the back and gently rubbing his shoulders. He looked up at her and she smiled into his eyes. Richard followed the urge to lean forward and kiss the first girl of his life—a kiss that was not refused, but accepted and returned with vigor. She was smaller than the other girls, but still larger than Richard. She held his head in her hands and guided his lips around hers. It was not unpleasant, and Richard was not afraid.

****

The Nancy Boys marched, wickedly out of formation, and twirling their small bats they quietly opened the bar door and shuffled inside. They advanced on the kissing pair—Bunny was on top of Richard, tenderly holding him down. Richard was in ecstasy. He was letting himself be devoured by her lips, and he opened his eyes for only a second to see if the kiss was really true, when a boldly tasseled chiffon-black arm swung through the air and a junior Louisville Slugger slammed into the right side of Bunny's face. The Boys swarmed about her like a sadistic flock of hummingbirds.

"NOOOO!" Richard screamed. "NOT HER! NOOOO!"

But it was too late, the rage of a thousand tiny cocks exploded in Bunny's direction—she was being beaten, almost savagely. Richard struggled to help her, but he was quick hustled out the door and toward the waiting cars. The Boys were merciless with Bunny, well, as merciless as they were capable of, which meant a few hard swings and then a hasty retreat—their soft slippers making no sound on the beer and yeast-soaked floor.

Richard was wrapped in a light cream-colored robe of soft terrycloth and placed into the backseat of the long black sedan. Against his protestations, he was comforted by members of his gang—one Boy on each side—stroking and fawning over the trembling man. The other Nancys soon followed suit, running from the bar, and leaping into the waiting vehicles.

The rescue procession was just pulling away when the barroom door opened and Ida and Margaret burst out. They were furious, fists clenched, shaking great sleepy arms in the air. Richard couldn't hear their curses but he could feel their heat through the rear window of the limo, and then Bunny limped from the club, holding a bloody, wet rag to her face. Staggering, she reached a hand toward the car and Richard wistfully looked back, his heart fiercely beating. The Nancys drove away.

****

The Boys brought Richard to a neat penthouse apartment on the corner of Broadway and 7th. There they bathed him and washed away the outer disgrace of his torment. They did not pry. The Boys compassionately waited for Richard to speak.

"It was horrible," he said. "They beat me and they used me, but there was one, one girl, the one I kissed that was different. She was kind and gentle, loving and sweet—"

"And she was young," Tommy broke in, "and she was dangerous and got what she deserved."

"No," Richard argued, "she was different. She wasn't like them."

"Richard, you were hurt and confused. People do strange things under stress. I once dated a girl."

"*You did?*" The attending Nancy Boys asked in unison. Richard was intrigued. "Yes," Tommy continued, "and she was like your girl, she was sweet and kind at first, we even slept together, once, but she got older, and wider, and less put together, and then one day she changed, just like yours would. It was her nature Richard, and as sweet as you thought she was you can't go against nature. Let it go, stay here where you're loved and protected—where you belong." Tommy stroked

Richard's hair and then gently squeezed his neck. "There's a great new DJ at the hotel, and after a few cosmos you'll forget all about those nasty old things and this terrible day."

Richard leaned against Tommy and smiled—the silk pant-leg of Tommy's slacks felt cool and comforting against Richards face.

"You're right Tommy, I *was* confused and this is where I belong, with you, and the Boys."

Richard stretched his neck and soaked in the loving protection of the gang. He stood and the smart cut of his pajamas hung squarely off his shoulders—a beautiful Japanese silk.

"I am feeling better," he said, "and maybe tonight, after a couple of cocktails, we could drive by that clubhouse and catch one of those bulls, give her a taste of what they gave me, a little retribution for their nasty ways—it's too bad though."

"What's too bad Richard?"

"It's too bad we're not beer drinkers."

"Ohhh," the Boys exclaimed in disgust. "Why?"

Richard reached out and lustfully stroked Tommy's cock through his slacks.

"Because, those cosmopolitans taste just as nice second hand."

Once Was an Angel

He'd been summoned a million times—humans, at the point of some near hurt or death, reaching out for help from beyond their world—and he'd responded. It was the duty of his kind to walk these streets, serve these beasts—these mutant children of God—and Darius, the Angel, had grown to resent it.

"Why should I serve them?" he questioned. *"Why is my life about doting at the hands of these... these weak men? I'm equal to God in their world, and yet, I'm no better than a slave."*

On this fall afternoon, Darius had been summoned to the Seaside rest home near the ocean, on the shore.

"Yes," he giggled, *"the shore marking the end of your short pathetic lives."*

Darius was tall; his skin a deathly blue-marble white and, from his back, rose great magnificent wings that, when unfurled, spanned the length of two men. His tail nimbly swung behind him as he walked the rest home hall; it bounced from wall to wall. There was a wheelchair blocking his way, so he gave it a slight shove—its elderly occupant barely startled by the unseen force that rocketed his senility down the hall and into an orderly's tray stacked with easy-to-digest meals.

"This place reeks of death," Darius said.

He dipped his finger into a vanilla pudding cup and then wriggled his long nose in disgust.

"Is this your idea of a joke," he glanced toward the heavens, "artificial manna, for the nearly deceased?"

Darius strolled into the room of an old woman and sat down on a chair near her bed—she was about to swallow a pill that would become lodged in her throat. Without Darius' help, she would surely perish.

"What's the point?" He pondered. *"Here she is, lying in her own filth a burden to her family, and of service to no one. She's a tax upon those around her, and yet..."* he looked above again. *"You want her around for what, another three or four days of worshipping you?"*

Darius leaned back in the chair and put his feet up on her bed. He was wearing shiny black leather boots that went remarkably well with his red, sharkskin suit.

"I think I'll let her die—watch her choke on the antidote to her ills."

He folded his arms and waited in patient repose.

The old woman, with skeletal hands, put the large white pill in her mouth and Darius watched with glee as her ancient old puss opened wide and then chomped down on her savior. She began to gasp—a wrinkled old fish flopping about on a yellowed Sear's Posturepedic mattress—fighting for breath. Darius was unmoved. He calmly spent a moment or two watching her suffer, and then instinctively he was forced to act. He materialized in front of the old woman, grabbed her head, and snaked his long tongue into her mouth, deep into the back of her throat where it roped the pill and brought it forth, saving her life. She exhaled a large dry dusty cloud of stale old woman breath— Darius retched.

"What the fuck?" he exclaimed.

He shoved the old woman down on the bed and jumped on top of her—sitting on her hips, riding her like a flipped over nag. He roughly grabbed her ears and pulled her pruney face close to his—her old bones painfully popped and cracked.

"Do you know where you are, mother?" he hissed at her.

"Do you like this?"

He released his tongue and took a long wet swipe up her face. The old woman frozen to the sheets,—in static shock—this monster carnally real.

"What are you?" she croaked.

Darius lifted into the air above her.

"I'm death, you old fuck," Darius lied. *"But you're not worth killing. Enjoy your last, granny, and when you see Him, speak kindly of me."*

The angel laughed and vanished from the room.

****

"I'm telling you Zeke, I can't take it anymore. I think I'm losing it. I'm turning into a real vicious prick. And what's the point anyway, I mean really, you've been doing this as long as I have, don't you ever wonder why?"

Ezekiel took a quick glance around the office.

"I'm wondering why you're still here Darius, why they haven't kicked your ass downstairs."

"You wanna know why?" Darius replied. "I'll tell you why. It's because I save lives, and after all isn't that what *He* wants—to rescue a woeful world of worshiping humans? Who cares what I say, or how I come off to those beasts, it's my actions that count, right? The humans say the road to hell is paved with good intentions—well my intentions might be evil, but last week I pulled close to five-thousand saves—that's why."

Darius took a sip from a cup of coffee that wasn't cold or bitter—even though it'd been sitting out for several hours—170 degrees, optimum temperature for that beverage. He spat it on the floor.

"Fuck!" he exclaimed, "How about a shitty cup of coffee once in a while? It's too fucking perfect here. I want a cloudy day when it's supposed to be bright; I want a storm when they've asked for calm. I'm done I tell you. I'm fucking done—and I hate serving them."

Ezekiel put his hand on Darius's shoulder. He was brotherly and kind, understanding and offered his support.

"Darius, shut up. Take what they give you. Do as you're told. And before you know it, it'll all be over. We've got another hundred years or so until He pulls the plug, and then you won't have to worry anymore. And believe me—if you think Lucifer's people have it any better, I can guarantee you that Baal is probably sitting down there right now wishing he could get a cup of warm Joe instead of that cold bitter crap they're serving below.

Darius gamely laughed. "Well," he said "I do like my cup warm."

Ezekiel began to shimmer... "I got a call Darius, I gotta go."

He disappeared.

****

Darius took the elevator to the first floor and checked in at angel resources. He wasn't surprised that this office had suddenly appeared, or that angel resources now existed when a moment before it hadn't, because that's how things were around here—if *He* thought you needed it, it appeared.

"Unless it was something that He didn't want to appear" Darius thought, *"and then you got shit."*

The heavenly system was aggravating to Darius, but he wandered up to the counter and checked in. The angel behind the desk was new. Darius didn't know her, and he wasn't too interested in small talk.

"I need to see somebody," Darius demanded, "maybe, a shrink, or something? Do you have that sort of thing here?"

"Yes, Darius," she politely replied. "The doctor has been waiting for you. Go in."

Darius purposefully sat in the doctor's red leather chair rather than on the long couch that he knew was designated as the patients' spot."

The doctor, without argument, calmly sat on the sofa. He was everything a psychiatrist should be—if you were thinking of one; white hair framing an old man's face, silver-grey neatly trimmed beard, small, round eyeglasses with gold wire frames, and a long, clean white coat. The bluish skin and tended wings of an angel were also as Darius expected—he surely would not seek help from a human.

"Do you feel better now?" the doctor asked. "Are you relieved?" Darius was confused.

"I just got here," the angel said, in a less than kind voice. "*What do you mean do I feel better*? You just barely opened your mouth."

"Well," the doctor casually replied. "You came in and sat in the chair you knew must be for me, so that had to give you a feeling of control—and even, if I dare say so, a certain sense of defiance and superiority. Isn't that what you're seeking? Do you feel satisfied?"

Darius stood and walked to the couch.

"Get up," he ordered. He pointed at his recently vacated chair. "Let's go Freud." He snapped his fingers and the doctor without a word switched places with Darius.

The angel felt his anger rise. "No more games," he said. "I'm uncomfortable, and I want help."

"Whatever you say, *Darius*," the doctor replied. "Now, what brings you here?"

The angel sat for a moment, he wasn't exactly sure why he was there, and there really wasn't any precedent for this type of thing. As a matter of note, Darius wasn't sure if an angel had ever sought help before—especially, help of this nature.

"You're troubled Darius," the doctor said. "Let it out. Go ahead, you can talk here."

"Okay," Darius responded, "You wanna talk? I'll talk. I'm down there pulling wrinkled old crones out of the frying pan, for what? Who gives a fuck? Where do they even go when they die? You ever see one around here? And, for that matter, I'm sick of it. I'm tired of serving them, and I'm not gonna do it anymore."

The doctor smiled. "I understand, Darius."

"*You understand?*" The angel was furious. "*Who the fuck are you?* Are you down there, digging in that human shit? I don't smell the scent of man on you—have you ever even seen one? They're horrible. Do you know I almost let one die? Yeah, don't look so shocked—400,000 years of half-monkey ass wiping and I'm over it."

"Darius, have you ever felt for one of them?"

"What?" Darius questioned. "I'm telling you how I feel right now."

"No," the doctor said. "Have you ever cared?"

"Cared about what?" Darius asked.

"Their struggles, their pain, their loss—have you ever looked into their eyes when they break, it's beautiful."

"They're nothing." Darius replied. "You're asking me if I care for *things*—as if they're in some way different from this coat or these pants I wear. When they're done, just like my trousers, they're done. I get new ones. There's a seemingly unending stream of human filth that populates that planet, and you're asking me *if I grieve for them, if I feel loss, or want?* What are you fucking talking about? Exactly what are you saying?"

"Darius, He's very concerned about you—we're all concerned about you."

"Concerned about me? Then why does He have me serving those fucks, those dull, dim-witted beasts? What the fuck do they ever do for Him? What do they do now, huh? Did you know that some of us call them the dream-wreckers? Have you seen what they've done down there? They've made a mess of it."

"Darius, please, I know they're difficult—*He* knows they're difficult, but He was hoping that maybe, after all this time, you might…"

"I might what; learn to take it up the ass with a smile on my face?"

The doctor laughed, "Darius, I'm going to let you in on a secret, something that only a few of us know. God screwed up."

"What?" Darius asked. He leaned forward on the couch.

"He screwed up." The doctor continued, "Do you want to know why you're angry, why you don't see how He could care, and why you hate *them* so much? It's because He didn't create you with a built-in ability to love. You have to learn it, and you haven't—and when you don't have it, you sure as hell can't see it in anyone else, let alone them. Why do you think Lucifer had such a hard time? He didn't love either. Darius, when you were created, He forgot to put love in you, all he gave you was a desire to serve, and after a while, service without love becomes slavery. No wonder you're angry, no one wants to be a slave, especially an angel."

Darius sat quietly. Not a thought crossed his mind—he was stunned to silence. After a moment, the doctor spoke again.

"*He* loves them Darius, and that's all you need to know."

There was a moment of heavenly quiet.
"Are you fucking kidding me?" Darius broke the stillness in the room. "This is the help I get? *He loves them—you don't?* I'm supposed to just run back there and keep it up? I won't do it. I'm not taking another fucking call."

"Well, you could learn how to love," said the doctor. "That would make the service and the understanding easier, but that hurts, too. If I were you, I'd just shut up, and keep serving. Listen to your friend Ezekiel, and if you get a little loose with a few of the humans, so what." The doctor smiled, "I'm sure *He'll* forgive you."

Darius began to shimmer—he was being called and there was nothing he could do about it.

"Nice talking with you, Darius—have a great day."
Darius and the doctor disappeared.

****

It was another random save, a young human child thoughtlessly ran in front of an auto. Darius did his job—sort of. He saved the child from dying, but he did let the boy get hit, and he laughed as the young body cart-wheeled across the intersection. Darius caught the child's head before it bounced off the pavement, and miraculously—according to the human witnesses—the boy walked away relatively unharmed, save for a few minor scratches.

"I don't get it," Darius complained to himself after the rescue, "this love thing. I would have thought that if He really loved the kid He would have had me kill the driver—or at least stop the boy from darting in front of a car. Love," he sighed. "What is love anyway, an emotion in which you let the failings in others fade into non-existence? Is that what love is? That you care nothing about their frailties and their weaknesses, and you ignore the fact that they just aren't good enough or strong enough to exist? Where is the perfection in that? Where is the glory in loving those who are not fit to be loved? I cannot learn to lessen myself, so that those beneath me may rise."

Darius moved among the people—unseen, unsettled, and gliding in no heavenly rhythm. He stopped on the corner of 51st and Bay, hovered over the street, and watched as a herd of men crossed on the green light. The city air was soiled with their petty conversations, deep clouds of black thought, pain rising from their minds and drifting toward their Maker...

"They are nothing more than fearful beasts," Darius thought, as he listened to their minds. "Or maybe, they're just sad tortured little clowns created perfectly for the amusement of Him," he smirked, "Our most wonderful Lord."

A young woman on crutches hobbled past Darius—her deformity, twisted and warped.

"Really?" Darius said. He reached out and touched the rough curve of her spine as she passed. "He loves this—how quaint."

Darius drifted to the ground then held up his hand, palm out, his long fingertips reaching toward the stars. A man stopped before him. He wore the uniform of a city worker—orange jumpsuit, pants cuffed over thick black rubber boots. The man had recently been in the sewer, so his hands were foul with the grime that lay beneath the streets. He couldn't see the obstruction of Darius—he thought he had paused to think and rest—but his mind was displayed like a vibrant life painting pinned to the corners of the city street, shamelessly unfurled before the angel.

"What could He possibly see in one so foul?" Darius wondered. "It surely cannot be in their looks." The angel pushed the man's greasy hair away from his face and then wrapped it in his fist and held him still. "Their works have brought no joy to this world. They may at times comfort each other, but they do so to heal wounds that they themselves brought on. I will give no praise to those who take pride in softening a harm that others of their kind created—they are all guilty, and not one rises above the rest."

Darius looked into the man—the worker was troubled, worried about his daughter. She was in poor health, plagued by the evils in her mind, melancholia, hysteria. Darius followed the man's thoughts as they led through the city and into the bedroom of the young girl. She was asleep in the man's dream, drugged and resting quietly—the only time she seemed at peace.

120

Darius held the thought in place and then stepped through the man's mind into the bedroom of the girl. It was exactly as her father pictured—a young maid's room—pink, and fairy light, the only hint to the madness lying under the covers was a stack of paintings on the desk—brilliant, tortured, oil-colored-static, reflecting the terrors of her dreams. Darius was surprisingly and uncharacteristically moved.

"Maybe it's all this talk of love," he thought, *"but I can almost feel her pain."*

He lifted the painting and admired the strokes drawn by her trembling hand—a seascape aswim with death and loss. *"She paints like an angel. Look how she's captured the essence of the ocean, the unselfish dangers of the sea."*

Darius lifted another, and then held still as death, for there, splashed across the piece, in fire blues and deep sea greens, were his eyes. The very likeness of Darius, chained to the canvas.

"What madness is this?" he questioned. *"What trick of God comes here?"*

Darius cocked his head in wonder, and then worriedly glanced about. *"This painting could mean trouble. I could be watched from on high. It does happen, not as much as one might think, but sometimes God does take an interest in those who serve him. The doctor did say they were worried, and if that were the case, there could be another angel following my path."* Darius instantly transported himself to the street, and then in a flash to the roof, the hallway outside the door, and then, the closet next to her bed, but there was no one there... he was alone, except for the girl lying silently beneath the flowered covers. Darius spoke out, just in case.

"Yes, I do dislike them," Darius admitted aloud, "but I enjoy this job, and I'm really going to try and learn this 'love' thing—it sounds like a great idea." Darius, amidst all his grumblings, did not want to be sent down—it was the coffee that did it. *"I'd rather be unhappy with a sweet, warm cup,"* he reasoned, *"than unhappy with a bitter, cold one."*

Darius, now satisfied that he'd covered his angelic ass, walked to the bed and gently lifted the blanket. She was sleeping on her stomach—her face buried in the pillows—so he reached down and tenderly put his hand under her chin, and lifted her face toward him. Her skin—teen-age blemished-alabaster—radiated a translucent light, which in spite of her illness lit the room like a candle that lay upon the breast of God. Darius found himself entranced by the girl. She was beautiful—a human carved from the ripe flesh of madness. Suddenly, she opened her eyes and Darius, trapped by her gaze, was visible to the girl and her eyes echoed the desperation of young love.

"Oh…" The angel exhaled what could only be described as the noise of a small pain, but in an instant the heaviness of the world descended upon him and he was crushed by its weight. He became solid, dropped to the ground, and was stranded on earth in his heavenly form—an angel, broken, pulled by his newfound love through the gates of heaven and dumped on the soft pile carpeting of a young girl's room.

She sat upright in her bed, her long red hair flowing over the sheets that she'd shyly pulled to her chin. With eyes surrounded by dark fields of unrested skin, she looked over her bedside and stared down at the figure of Darius.

"Hello?" she quietly called out. "Man? Are you okay?"

Darius was dazed—he felt heavy, and struggled to lift his head. He was unaccustomed to the weight of his now physical self. A bird fallen from the nest, he floundered.

"Man?" She called again. "Are you okay?"

"Help," Darius whispered. "Help me, please."

The girl didn't move—the shadows of her illness painted circles around the brilliant green windows of her soul, deathly shadows.

"Please," Darius begged. He managed to raise his arm. He reached for her.

The girl climbed naked from her bed. She was seventeen, barely a woman, and due to her mental illness she was more child than adult, but she knelt beside Darius and helped him sit up. He wasn't as heavy as he looked, and the angel, slowly gaining strength, wrapped his great wings around the girl and pulled her close. It was the first time that he'd ever tenderly held a human, and the scent of her—the sweet perfume of her sweat—was intoxicating. Darius stuck out the tip of his tongue and gingerly tasted her skin. She was clean and slightly salty, but when he slid his tongue down under her arm he grimaced and shook his head—her deodorant was metallic and unpleasant to his mouth.

"I know you," the girl said—she was not afraid of the angel; if anything, his appearance was a strange comfort to her and she laid her head against his chest. "I paint pictures of you," she told him, "there, on the desk. You've come to me at night. You're an angel."

Darius said nothing. He'd never been here before, and he wasn't sure how she knew him, but he let his hands roam freely over the girl's flesh. The new sensation of her skin thrilled him, and there was no place on her that he did not touch. Each sweet inch he ingested in his mind, memorizing the slight curves of her breasts, the territory of her self.

"Are you real?" she asked, doing nothing to stop his hands.

"I'm not sure what you mean by real," Darius answered, and then he remembered her illness. "I am here with you in this place, and I am flesh. This is no dream to be broken—I can bleed."

Darius lifted his hand to his mouth and bit through the skin. He had never bled before, but he held the wound toward the girl—bright red drops cascading to the carpet. She grabbed his hand, covered the wound with her mouth and suckled the blood until it stopped. She smiled up at Darius with lips now stained.

"Are you mine?" she asked.

The concept of ownership was unfamiliar to Darius, but he knew that these humans often attached to one another and, when he searched inside himself, the thought of being owned by this young girl was not strange or unpleasant.

"Yes," Darius said hesitantly, and then wholeheartedly, "I will be yours."

The girl leaned against him and they held each other—as mother and daughter, father and child, lover against lover—their bodies locked in that tight embrace punctuated only by slight hand movements and flutters as they secured and then readjusted their holds. For some time they sat, oblivious to the world around them. Darius grew strong.

The girl lovingly pulled away and then looked into his eyes.

"Can I see you?" she asked, as she started unbuttoning his shirt—her nimble fingers working on the fine black silk. "I've never seen a man without his clothes. You are a man, too, aren't you?"

Darius wasn't sure. He was not himself, but he was not her either. He lifted the girl from him and then raised himself to his full height. He was seven feet tall, a span meant to symbolize an arm of God, one-third of a Holy image. He kicked off his shoes and then removed his coat, shirt and pants. He stood naked before the girl, then shook and spread his wings—the tips of which reached from wall to wall.

The girl, still unclothed, moved closer to Darius and held her hands out to him. She touched the angel's chest and then attentively slid her fingers down to his hips. She placed her hand on the smooth mound between the angel's legs.

"I don't think you're quite a man," she told him. "You don't have anything, here." She gently stroked. "You're like a doll," she said, "a great, blue doll."

Darius felt proud. He could sense delight in her assessment of him. "Do you have a name?" She asked. "I'm Emily."

She held out her small hand. Darius reached out and gently wrapped her hand in his.

"Emma-Lee-Graves—Emily for short," she said.
"I am Darius," the angel replied. "This name comes with nothing else, and it's not too short, just Darius, as it's been forever."

"*Darius...*" she whispered, caressing the name with her lips, "I like it. Will you stay here with me?"

The angel thought for a moment. Could he still move, could he fly? Darius concentrated on the street outside. He closed his eyes and imagined himself standing on the pavement looking back at the girl's house, but when he reopened them he was still there—naked, standing on the carpet.

"Yes," he said. "I will stay with you."

"Forever?" She asked hopefully.

"Yes," pledged Darius, "I think I will stay forever."

Emily smiled and walked over to the nightstand, reached for a small metal box.

"I like my songs sad, sweet, and full of love, like a warm night rain falling on the flowers outside." The angel watched as she held the shiny rectangle in her left hand, the fingers on her right gliding across a smooth glass face, spinning around a dial. She found what she was looking for, "Last Goodbye" and set the small box down.

"I love to dance, Darius."

Instantly, music filled the room and to Darius it was beautiful, just as she said. He could feel the pain emanating from the vibrations of the song, but also, there was hope, the sadness wasn't futile or depressed, it was... Darius searched for the words... "It was a kiss goodbye." He'd seen it before, two humans when they separate, pushing their lips together, then breaking their connection, and yet, in some way, celebrating their love at the same time. Darius watched Emily move. She swayed with the music, reminding him of the night flowers. She'd become one of them, moving in the torn breeze of the sound. Emily danced toward Darius. She took his hands and encouraged him to move, to sway like she did. The angel closed his eyes and imagined he was her, moving across the carpet

128

swaying in rhythm, a flower in the night, and then he too moved with the song. Emily sang along with the words, and through her Darius began to understand the beauty in the pain...

"Just hear this and then I'll go. You gave me more to live for... more than you'll ever know."

"*It is loss,*" Darius thought. "*But it's finding, too. This song is as beautiful as she is, as imperfect.*

Yes, her skin is blemished and her mind touched, true, but I love her, and even more so because she is flawed. She is the rain, she is my storm and my sun, I love her beauty and I love her disease. She is everything to me; she is my reason to live, my reason to..."

"EMILY!" The door to the room had opened and there, standing in the doorway, was her father—the worker from the city.

"GET AWAY FROM IT!" He yelled.

Her father ran toward the couple, pushed at Darius and grabbed the girl's arm. He tried to pull her away, but the angel did as he had for thousands of years—he instinctively reached out, and he saved her. Darius grabbed the girl's father by his neck, and he broke him. He had been a large man but he was no match for the angel—he fell lifeless to the floor.

Darius calmly kept dancing.

"DADDY!" The girl screamed and dropped next to

her father. "DARIUS!" She yelled. "WHAT DID YOU DO?"

Darius opened his eyes and stopped swaying.
"I saved you," Darius calmly replied. "I love you." He beamed

at the girl, ignoring the body on the floor.

"HELP ME!" She screamed. She tried lifting her father but his head fell forward on to his chest, his neck was snapped at the base. "Darius," she stood and pulled at the angel. "Do something!"

Darius walked over and lightly prodded the body with his foot. "I can't," he said. "He's not in there. I'm not sure where they go, but he's not in there."

"Darius, what are you saying?"

"There's no one there." He kicked at the body again, "It's...it's...nothing." Darius closed his eyes and swayed.

"WHAT ARE YOU DOING?" She screamed.

"I'm moving, dancing like you do. Come with me." He held out his hands, pulling the girl to her feet.

"STOP IT!" She yelled. She was panicked now, darting back and forth between Darius and her father. "Help me!"
"I did help you." Darius said. "I helped us. He's gone. We can dance now, and we can kiss." He reached for her again but then, the music stopped. Darius wanted more.

Emily grabbed her phone and dialed the number for the police. Darius grabbed the small metal box and attempted to restart the song.

"9-1-1, what is your emergency?" The voice was professional, calm. "Please," she yelled. "He killed my father! Help me! Help me!"

Darius held the metal box toward her.

"*Help me*," he said. "Could you make the sounds come again? Are they in there, too?" Darius leaned over and tried to put his ear to her phone.

"Hello?" The emergency operator said. "Are you there?"

Emily yanked the phone away. "Help!" She yelled. She backed away from Darius—he followed.

"Please, Emily," Darius grinned, "the song."

The girl grabbed the box and hit replay. The song flared to life. Darius stopped then swayed.

"Hello..." the operator said, "...are you there?"
"I'm here! I'm here!" Emily yelled. She ran from the room.

"Miss, I need you to calm down. Where are you? Is the assailant still there?" The operator was firm, professional.

"Yes," Emily cried. "He killed my father! Help!"

"We have officers on the way. Stay on the phone with me until they arrive."

Darius felt sad when Emily left the room—it was almost as if the sun now refused to shine. He wanted a kiss goodbye as, *"that's what lovers do when they leave, they kiss goodbye."* He followed. Darius wandered down the hallway and into the living room of her small house, calling her name.

Emily was still on the phone. Darius came toward her.

"I want a kiss," he said, "a sad, pretty kiss goodbye."

"Stay away from me!" She yelled as she backed toward the front door of the house. Darius continued moving toward her.

"But I miss you when you're gone. I love you Emily!"

"Go away, I hate you! You're a monster. You killed my father."

Darius started to cry. He reached up and touched his cheek, felt the wetness, and caught a tear on his finger which he brought to his mouth. He tasted it; it was salty like she was. He held his tear-stained finger out to her. "Look how I hurt. Look Emma Lee Graves, Emily for short, look how I hurt."

The girl, still naked, went through the door to the outside and Darius followed

"I forgive you," he said. "I know you don't mean it—you love me too."

A police cruiser pulled up to the house, then another and another. Officers jumped from their cars, guns drawn and pointed at the naked angel. The girl ran toward them. Darius stood tall, still crying.

"Get down on the ground," an officer ordered, but the angel would not stop. He advanced toward the girl, toward the officers, toward their guns. "Stop!" The officer shouted. "We will shoot."

Darius wiped another tear from his cheek and, carefully balancing it on his finger, he held it out and continued toward the girl. "Look Emily, look at me hurt."

The first bullet tore through his chest, the second his stomach—

the third, fourth, and fifth, back to his chest. Darius dropped to his knees—the warm day breeze weaved its way through the holes in his body.

"I love you Emily," he gasped as he pledged, "I love you."

He crawled toward her, tried to rise, but was hit by shots six and seven, two more—one exploding his knee, the other tumbling through his shoulder slightly under his wing.

Darius collapsed. He was conscious for a moment and then the world wavered and became still.

"Darius… Darius? Can you hear me?" It was Ezekiel. "Are you done now? Have you had enough?"

"Oh," Darius sighed, "Please don't take me. I love her."

Ezekiel looked down at his friend's body as the police advanced with Taser and club.

"It's time to go Darius," he said. "Come on."

Ezekiel held out his hand and reluctantly Darius grabbed it. The angels vanished.

****

"So that's love, huh?" Darius asked. "It was awful."
"Yeah," Ezekiel said, "I could have told you that, but you wouldn't listen."

"You know," Darius went on. "Maybe He didn't give us that ability on purpose, maybe He didn't fuck up. Maybe, He did it to protect us."

"Maybe who did it?" Ezekiel asked. "Did what? What ability? What are you talking about?"

"I'm talking about love. The doctor said He screwed up, didn't give us the ability to love, and that's why I was so angry. He said I was a slave."

"And you believed him?"

"Yeah, of course I did, why not?"

"I'll tell you Darius, you may do great works but you're a fool of the highest order—tricked into love and too blind to see it."

"He was a doctor with an office and a couch, he told me so."

Ezekiel smiled, "And to Adam he was a snake, and to Christ he was a word. Have you been back to see her, checked in on her, cruised by her bed at night?"

Darius hung his head. "Yes," he said. "I was thinking that maybe if I tried again, was a little more understanding, softer, or kind, that maybe things might work out."

"Darius, you murdered her father. She called the police on you. They tried to kill you."

"Yeah, she did," Darius sheepishly replied, "but she said she loved me, and she looks so beautiful when she dances."

Ezekiel began to shimmer. "I've got to go; I've got a call to take, but Darius…"

"Yeah, Zeke?"

"I love you," laughing as he disappeared.

A Late Night Session

It wasn't a loud knock, more like a tap-tap really, but it was enough to get me out of bed and opening the front door. At first I thought it was a prank, some errant children playing late-night door ditch-'em games, for when I looked out no one was there—at least no one at eye, or even waist level—and I was about to withdraw, shut the door, and head back to bed, when a voice, a small, cute, cuddle-me-up-on-the-blanket voice, spoke from below my knees. It was a rabbit—a stuffed child's toy standing all white fur distressed on my porch.

"May I?" The bunny quietly asked as it stepped into my home. "It's frightfully cold outside, and he's being most impolite—terribly so."

The bunny was soft white fur with deep brown eyes, and it looked as if it'd been crying; the fur on its cheeks was tear-stained and matted.

"We need help," the bunny continued "and you've come recommended, highly recommended."

I was a therapist—a family counselor—but I didn't work with toys.

I started to shut the door when another voice came from outside—it was a deep voice, a scuffed up, rascally voice.

"I told her it wasn't true, but she wouldn't listen—never listens, unless it's something that she thinks she wants to hear." I looked outside and the voice was coming from a bear; a two-foot tall, overstuffed teddy, laboriously making his way, one stuffed leg at a time, up the stairs from my yard.

"This was her idea," he continued, "not that I'm against it, but I told her, '*if you'd just listen to me, we wouldn't have to be out on a night like this.*' "

He was very chatty for a bear and the night, as he called it, was not pleasant—it was a desperate evening of wind and threatening rain. I held the door, and he too crossed the threshold of my home.

140

"I, I don't normally see people at night," I stuttered.

The bear growled, "But we're not people, and we only come out at night. How would it be, the two of us," he gestured towards the bunny, "walking about in broad daylight with her crying and complaining? I don't see what help you're going to be if you can't even reason that out."

"I'm not saying…"

"He's not saying anything at all Bear, because he has no voice," the bunny interjected, "You won't let *him* speak, just as you won't let *me* speak. You don't want me to be what I am. You don't want me to have a voice!" The bunny started crying as she went on, "You just want a body, a warm body to cuddle against. But I'm more than that… I'm so much more."

The bear hung his head, mumbled a slight apology and then looked up at me with green button eyes—the right eye chipped and broken. This was an older bear, a bear with plenty of before-bedtime roughhousing on him—a used bear.

"No problem," I said as I led them deeper into my home. "We can sit here, anywhere you like."

I had a small room that I used for my clients, the walls painted a calm goldenrod with a few fake palms, and an over-stuffed couch and chair. It was a comfortable room, a room to relax in and let go. The bunny and the bear sat next to each other on the sofa—a pillow placed between the two, separating them. The bear looked nervous. He was obsessively running his paw over the arm of the couch, pushing and squeezing the sofa.

"Are you comfortable?" I asked him.

"Yes, comfortable," he said. "I was just wondering what kind of stuffing you have in this couch." He glanced longingly down at his arm which was slightly torn and seemed to have lost a bit of its filling. "It's very nice," he continued, as he rubbed the sofa, "very nice."

"So, what brings the two of you here?" I asked.

"That's just it," the bunny cried. "It's not 'two', it's one. It's always him, him, him. I'm nobody when he's around." The bunny spoke in a voice that reminded me of an Indian-summer bell—a beautiful voice.

"You're not nobody; you're Bunny," the bear grumbled under his breath. "*You think you're nobody*, that's the problem."

The bunny looked at me sad-eyed while pointing accusingly at the bear. "He's not a therapist, if anything he's a hypnotist—a charmer. Don't listen to him. He lies and people believe him. They always believe him. Nobody ever believes me."

"That's not true," The bear replied. "I don't lie. Well, I do lie, but I don't lie about the things that matter, I don't lie about the truth."

The bear *was* strangely believable.

"You see," the bear rumbled on, "she does these things and then blames me. She was shuffled from child to child and she never got close to anyone. I listen to her. I beg her to speak. She blames me for a lifetime of what others did. I'm not a monster. I'm a bear. A big cuddly bear, and I just want to love her, but she's making it most difficult."

The bunny had been quiet as the bear spoke, but now she shook and shivered with anger on the couch.

"He's a liar!" she yelled. "I saw him! He was on her bed, the older girl, and he was nestled in her arms snuggling, and cuddling. She kissed him, right on the lips! And he let her!"

"I did not!" the bear roared. He stood up on the couch and held his great big paws aloft, looming over the bunny in a most threatening way. "You're the one!" He growled. "Where did all those little bunnies come from? There was just you and now there are bunnies everywhere—hundreds of bunnies on the bed!"

The bear lumbered towards her. "STOP!" I yelled. "Stop it!"

He held his place but he turned and looked at me with a savage forest stare. It was unsettling and I was afraid.

"Please," I said, "please Mr. Bear, be calm and breathe. Please."

The bear settled and then plopped down on his well-padded bottom. He slowly, resignedly shook his head.

"I know what she is," he said softly, "and I don't mind her nature, if only she would not mind mine. She can't help herself, try her."

"What?" I wasn't sure what he meant.

"Try her." He turned toward the bunny.

I looked at her and her face had changed. Her eyes slowly swirled with lust. She leaned back on the couch and seductively spread her legs.

"Touch her," the bear coaxed. "Go ahead, touch her."

I was strangely compelled to lean over, and I ran my hand along the side of her face—gently stroking her fur. She pushed into me.

"Hold her," the bear commanded.

I picked up the bunny and held her against my face. She nuzzled into my neck and tiny-bunny-kissed my cheek.

"Take me," she purred, and there was something of her that made me want her—an attraction that went beyond anything I'd ever felt. I needed her and I didn't care that the bear was watching—standing now on the sofa, intent on our contact, directing our play. I put the bunny in my lap and she wiggled against me—moving her hips as a woman would, but with more desire and purpose.

"Let me hold her for you." The bear climbed down from the sofa and grabbed the bunny. He carried her to the couch and laid her on her back—her legs spread, eyes closed.

"Do it," he said. "She wants this, this is what she's made for."

I undid my pants and got down on my knees before the pair. I held her small legs apart and I pushed against her, then into her. She was warmer and more comforting then any woman I'd ever had.

"Bite me," the bunny whispered to the bear. The bear leaned down, kissed her, and lightly bit into her neck. "Watch me Bear," she purred, "watch me."

The bear watched as the bunny opened herself more—I pushed deeper, moving with her, letting her guide me with her hips, grinding slowly against me, and then I quickly came, releasing into the toy.

The bunny leaned back and passionately kissed the bear and he returned her kiss in kind. I was dazed, unbelieving, and thoroughly confused. The bunny pulled away from me and sat back on the couch, calm, relaxed, and cuddling against the bear.

"I'm sorry." I said, suddenly embarrassed. "I... I don't know what came over me. I'm sorry."

"It's okay," said the bear. "She's a good bunny, but she's a bunny, and I don't blame her for that—as long as she doesn't blame me for being a bear." He picked the bunny up and walked towards the door, carrying her gently in his arms. The bunny looked relaxed and tired, like a child peacefully falling asleep.

"You were very good," the bear said to me, "and we'll be back—it won't be long before she gets troubled again, so we'll need your help."

The bear put the bunny over his shoulder, opened the door, and stepped outside. The bunny looked back and then opened her mouth to speak.

"He's a very naughty bear, a hypnotist bear, and I told you not to believe him. I'm a good little bunny, and he never lets me speak."

The bear closed the door behind him and they walked off into the night.

Something to Burn

When the grocery store on South Spring turned to ashes in the parking lot, Terrance was across the street sipping on a soft drink soda and fiddling with the radio station. His car was without tape or CD capabilities, and probably as he figured, one of the last vehicles to come off the assembly line with only an AM/FM player—"Do you know how hard it is to find the proper arson-accompanying music on commercial radio?" He had flipped through numerous channels, even trying a few of the Mexican stations, before he finally settled on a late night talk show. He didn't care what they were going on about—politics mostly—but the monotonous, deep, comforting voices sounded real cool as he watched the store implode. It was like a live TV news report—sans anchor, with a burning building in the background.

Terrance had a feeling that this fire was going to be good, and it didn't disappoint. You see, although the building was in a shopping mall, it stood apart from the other stores—plenty of room on both sides for ventilation, and lots of windows; the more windows the better. It was nice to be able to look inside while that rambunctious little flame so rudely danced down the aisles tickling the canned goods on number nine before leaping over to aisle twelve and disintegrating the laxatives and the foot powder. There is nothing more satisfying than seeing your handiwork come to life, and Terrance had been satisfied many times—three times this month, and it had always been uplifting. But now, he was beginning to get a trifle bored—the newlywed shine was wearing off the flames and he thought it might be nice to step it up a notch, add a new element; perhaps insert a figure or two into the picture—a *ménage à trois* of sorts. "How would it be," he wondered, "to watch a man run about trying to escape the flames—or a woman for that matter? How long would it take before they went the way of the tissues and the frozen foods?" It was an exciting thought. Terrance sat back in his seat and tapped his fingers on the steering wheel—"burn, baby, burn."

Terrance hoped that tonight's view would be a clear one, and he'd gotten his wish. The flame danced slowly for him, and the fire's lecherous patron—that cloud of loose smoke that hung around and tried to block his view of the action—was well behaved. He didn't mind the smoke, as long as it stayed on top, where it belonged, but when it filled the building, it was hard to see the burn; almost like a cherry on top of a sundae. "Cherry on top, that's right, you didn't want cherry all over, just on top—like smoke, on top where it belonged." He checked his watch and realized he was about forty minutes away from getting fired—that is, if he didn't get back to his job.

Terrance was a night watchman—not a security guard—let's make that perfectly clear. He despised authority, and anything to do with the law. "People should be free to come and go as they please," he thought, "but they should be watched." Terrance's job was perfect—paid shit, boring as hell if he stayed around, but wonderful for what he loved doing best—watching, and starting fires. How lucky for him that this type of employment actually contributed to his leisure time enjoyment. "That's a rare thing," Terrance wickedly smiled, "loving my job as much as I do, I should thank someone."

Terrance returned to his place of employment, Hedge's Storage Yard, where he drove to the back of the building. A car was there—a dark blue, Crown Victoria that did not belong in the lot, and it was occupied. Terrance, although not an abnormally agitated man became very concerned, he *had* been off premises and he didn't want to lose his situation. The last thing he needed was to have to find another job, at the very untalented and unemployable age of fifty-one. He thought of a thousand different excuses to explain his absence, including one where he actually defecated in his pants as a ruse—"No one questions a man's inability to perform when he's carrying a hot load in his slacks."

"But, maybe it wasn't a threat," Terrance thought. "This lone Sedan occupant might not be a company man at all. Maybe, it's just a drunk sleeping it off on a deserted blacktop hideaway. Yeah, that's what it is, a drunk, too inebriated to drive—the bars had just recently closed—this is when they come out. Yes, it's a drunk, and he would need to be watched."

In the space of a few moments Terrance had turned a perceived threat into an opportunity to use his night watchman skills. "I'll give the guy credit for not driving, but I'll be damned if he's going to lay up in here, puking and pissing in my lot."

Terrance pulled directly behind the blue Sedan and slammed on his brakes. He then power-jumped his way from the driver's seat, hitched up his smoke-saturated, yet still unsoiled, size 28 polyester patrol pants, stood as tall as his five foot six small-boned frame allowed, and made ready to watch. But she was out of the car before he could get settled, and she had a gun, Terrance did not.

"Nice night for it, huh?" she was calm—a quick mover, but calm—and less concerned with her .45 caliber hand accoutrement than Terrance was. It was the first thing he noticed, cold steel nestled casually at her waist. "Of course," she continued, "a quick burn in a light rain can also be quite stunning. What do you have," she glanced at her watch, "about twenty minutes before the day man gets here?"

Terrance said nothing. He was watching his job, and his life, quickly evaporate.

"Oh, don't get me wrong," She said, "I'm a big fan of your work. I especially loved what you did to the sporting goods on West 75th—now, *that* was nice."

150

"I'm sure I don't know what you're talking about," Terrance lamely argued, "I'm a watchman, a night watchman, and, uh, you shouldn't be here."

She advanced toward him and Terrance took a step back—she had at least four inches on him, and maybe fifty pounds.

"You're telling me where I should be, little man? If I were you, I'd be worrying about where *you're* going to be." She opened her jacket and flashed Terrance the badge she wore on her hip—neatly clipped to a thin black belt holding up her slacks. "It is slacks, isn't it?" Terrance wondered out loud. "Do women wear pants?"

Terrance caught his thoughts and apologized. "I'm sorry, I didn't mean anything. We're on the same team, right?" The woman laughed.

"Oh, you're on my team, are you?" She holstered her gun, tucking it under the upper left side of her black leather jacket. It was a nice coat, more tailored than he would've thought appropriate on an officer, and her breasts were large, barely concealed behind a button-down white blouse. "We'll see whose team you're on," she said. She pulled a pack of cigarettes from her coat pocket, opened them and placed one on top of the thick coating of bright red lipstick that adorned her mouth.

The cigarette sunk down into the glossy paste until it settled on her lip. She pulled out an old metal lighter, a Zippo, and brought it to the tip of the smoke, cupped it with her left hand and then spun her right thumb along the wheel—a smooth click and a flash. Terrance closed his eyes for a moment and then wishfully

inhaled the butane as he watched her hands glow. He unconsciously maneuvered himself to get a better look. She lit the smoke and then slowly pulled the lighter away, the flame hardly disturbed at all by the cool night air. Terrance followed the lighter with his eyes as she circled the still-burning tool down to her waist and then back up to her face where she snap-closed the top, killing the flame and leaving Terrance staring directly into her eyes. He floundered for a moment and then shook his head clear.

"Yeah," she said, "you really love it, don't you?" She took a deep lung-expanding drag and then exhaled a thick silver cloud in Terrance's direction where, untouched by the smoke, he coughed anyway.

"I'm... I'm sorry." He stuttered, "Are you an officer? Am I being charged with something?"

"I don't know," she gave a casual television cop reply, "maybe arson. How does that sound, little 'firebug?' "

"I... I didn't do anything," Terrance said, "I was here all..." "All night?" She cut him off. "Were you about to lie to me?" She closed the gap between them, extended her arm, and grabbed the back of his neck. Terrance tried to shrug her off but she was stronger. She pulled him close. Terrance could smell the smoke on her breath, the leather of her coat, and a light trace of perfume or body lotion on her skin. Her cold manicured nails pressed sharp into his flesh.

"You're not gonna do fuck-all." She said. "I've been watching you, and I know where you've been. You're in trouble Terrance. That is your name isn't it—T. Terrance Boyd? Was your father black? Because it sounds like you gotta bit of brother in you; do you?" She reached down to his crotch and squeezed. "Hey!" Terrance pushed her hand away. "What the fuck?"

"I thought you were on my team, baby?" She laughed. Terrance took another look down at her badge, this woman was certifiable, and she was armed. He sniffed the air searching for that too much to drink odor, but it wasn't there—again, just perfume.

"I bet you're wondering how I found you?" She said. Terrance wasn't though, he was wondering about his job, the burning end of her smoke, and whether she could zip that jacket up with all those titties underneath. Terrance had seen more fires than he had sexual action, and that crotch grab, while unexpected and a bit abrupt, was kind of exciting.

"It wasn't hard," she continued. "Guys like you love your work, and after a couple of burns, I started rolling on fire calls—big calls. We knew we had an arsonist, and I know guys like you get off on watching, so I'd roll on those calls and drive around—laid back, no hurry, I didn't own any of the buildings you were torching, so I wasn't in any real rush to stop you. I just watched, and I looked for you, watching. After a couple of fires, I saw you, sitting in that old Ford piece of shit with a grin on your face from ear to ear—a just-eaten-dinner satisfied grin, a grin that didn't belong in *that* car," she gestured to his '76 Fiesta. "I didn't need to look twice to know it was you. No one would sit in that thing and smile, if their mind wasn't occupied somewhere else—isn't that right, Terrance?" She was right, and

154

despite his fear of being arrested, the woman's warm breath and tight grip had caused Terrance to become erect—embarrassingly so.

"What do you want from me?" He asked. He put his hands in his pockets and pulled his pants away from his cock—he didn't have to pull far. "I just don't want any trouble." He said. "I want to be helpful and…" "…and not go to jail?" She asked. "Yeah," Terrance said. "I don't want to go to jail."

She let her cigarette drop. Terrance followed its descent until it met the ground with a small explosion of sparks. It was beautiful, *"Even on a small scale, fire can be so grand."*

She checked her watch again—a nice piece, looked expensive, a big dial—the kind of watch that was usually made for men, a man's watch.

"I'm going to do you a favor, 'little bug'. Would you like that?" She asked.

Terrance nodded.

"I'm gonna save your ass, but first, you're going to do something for me—you do *want* to be on *my* team, don't you?"

Again, Terrance nodded.

She pulled a slip of paper out of her jacket pocket and handed it to him, it had an address scrawled across it. "I want you to go check this out, see what you can do with it, there's a hill on the

top of Olive, two streets over—a vacant lot with a great view…
and, Terrance?"

"Yes…um…uh." He vainly searched for her name.

"Check it before Friday. I'll be back then," she opened her car
door and looked over her shoulder. "Move that piece of shit, and
don't wander off. I'm watching you."

She pulled out of the lot before the day man pulled in.

****

The neighborhood was nice with large, individually designed
houses and trees, lots of trees. Terrance had been through here
before. There was a time last summer when he'd thought about
doing a piece of work up here. He'd seen other fires tear through
these hillside neighborhoods great, big beautiful burns that took
days to extinguish, but at the time he was still fairly new and he
didn't want to be too bold. He thought it would be best to work
his way up, you know, not get ahead of himself, show a little
humility. *"These days people weren't willing to put the time in,
everybody wanted to be a big shot—burn the whole city down,
what was the matter with starting on a row of dumpsters or a
carport?"* That's what he'd done. Yeah, he'd thought about it,
but he'd driven through the neighborhood as a student, admiring
what could be, not as a brute looking for undeserved glory.

Terrance thought back to his first burn, it was a one-car

garage—part of an old abandoned house near the airport, and he was rewarded for his humility. It started as a small fire, but it went quick and it spread, enveloping two more houses and a corner market in its wake before they could stop it. As a special treat, the runway near the burn had to be closed. *"You see, you start off with a bit of humility and you get rewarded."*

But Terrance was past that now. He drove down the street as a master might; surveying the materials available before he began his creation.

The lot on Olive was just as she said; he had an unobstructed view across the gully to the back windows of Three-Thirty-Six Sand Canyon Drive—the address she'd given him. It was nice, a real clean setup. The house was perched on a steep hillside so there were stilts supporting the rear. *"How wonderful,"* Terrance thought. *"It was almost as if the architect wanted it to be torched, like it was all plumped up and perched on the hillside screaming, 'burn me, burn me, burn me!' It couldn't have been better ventilated."* Terrance wondered what it would look like when the stilts gave way—burnt through, and the house tumbled like a flaming wooden comet down the hillside.

"Yes," Terrance thought, *"this is going to be a real nice treat."* He'd momentarily forgotten about the threat of jail, or loss of job, the fantasy of the fire weaved its way through him. Terrance took a quick look around the neighbor's houses and saw nothing too troublesome—a couple of windows, sure—lot

of windows, but this *was* a pretty high-digit area, and he doubted whether anyone was too concerned about their neighbors. *"That was the good thing with these places—stuffy hill-dwellers with money who wanted to live with a 'close' but 'outside-the-city' feel. Most of them didn't talk much to their neighbors—it decreased the feeling of isolation, so nobody should be getting too nosey."*

Terrance was just about to pull away when a light came on. It was a rear bedroom and a young blonde had just entered followed by... *"Shit!"* Terrance exclaimed, *"it's her, the cop from last night."* Immediately Terrance's worries about jail and the reality of his situation flashed back into his head. *"Does she know I'm out here? Does she know I'm, watching?"* Terrance ducked down in his seat as if it would somehow make his car less visible, but if she looked out, he would be spotted for sure. *"Ahhhhhh,"* the young girl had walked to the window and pulled the drapes closed. He started his car and was just about to put it in gear when the curtains parted again, but now, instead of the young blonde standing there, it was her—the cop—that crazy bitch framed between the drapes, standing in the window looking in Terrance's direction. When she saw him, a smile slowly spread across her face, like a line of petrol carefully poured onto a bedspread. Terrance turned off the car and sat, a rodent caught in her sights.

She proudly pushed the curtains open and then she stepped away and lowered the lights. The room darkened to a soft evening glow. Terrance held. She returned to the window with the young girl in tow and they stood exactly where Terrance could see them—two, almost silhouettes, framed behind the glass. The cop pulled the girl close and kissed her—a deep soulful kiss that rooted Terrance to his seat. She then ran her hands down the girl's shoulders and started unbuttoning her blouse, removing it, and then unfastening the bra beneath.

Terrance watched as the cop stripped her naked and then knelt before her. She kissed the girl's stomach and then worked her way down between her legs.

"What the fuck?" Terrance was confused. "This bitch brings me out here to have me watch her go down on some chick?" Terrance started the car again but the crazy in the window heard his engine and held up her hand, wordlessly commanding him to stay in place. She didn't want him to leave. Terrance sat and watched as the cop took the young girl to what looked like completion and then the officer stood, moved to the window, and closed the drapes.

"OK," Terrance said to himself. "I'm fucked. This bitch is crazy. I gotta go... no, no, no... if I leave town she'll screw me, and I'm broke, fuck, I'm broke! I can't run, but she's gonna do me if I don't. She's crazy, really crazy. Does she even want the place torched? See, there are people like her, lots of people like her, who just want to fuck with people, she just wants to fuck with me, and she doesn't care. I wasn't hurting anyone. I certainly didn't hurt her, she even said it didn't hurt her, but now she's doing this, she's hurting me like this. She makes me see it, makes me sit here and I can't..."

"What the fuck are you doing?" The woman appeared at the driver's window startling Terrance out of his rambling monologue. "I was, I was checking it out, like you told me," Terrance stuttered.

"You were probably sitting out here jerking off, you creep," she reached through the window and grabbed at Terrance's crotch.

"Stop it!" He raised his voice. "What do you want from me? Why are you doing this? What do you want?"

"Ha!" She laughed. "Easy, Romeo, lighten up, I'm just having some fun, giving you a little show, and you know what I want from you; I want you to do the place, with her in it."

"What?" Terrance asked.

"You heard me." She said. "I want you to torch it. I don't care if the whole fucking hill goes with it, but I want it done— tomorrow."

"But I've never hurt someone," he said. "And you were just with her—isn't she your... your..." Terrance fought for the word. "My bitch?" The cop laughed. "She's a piece of ass, Terrance; a rich piece of ass, and I'm tired of it. I'm thinking I might switch teams, get me a little boy to play with, maybe you."

"You're sick," he said, "and you need help!"

"I need help? Fucking firebug burning up half of LA and you tell me I need help. Listen here little bug, I could've done you in that parking lot last night, blown your fucking brains all over the back of Hedge's, and I would've been a hero, 'Female cop shoots male arsonist.' "

She reached down and pulled the gun out of her waistband. "Is that what I should've done, blown your fucking head off? I still can you know, I can say you found out I was investigating you and you followed me here, to kill me. I saw you outside, snuck up on you, identified myself and you resisted. So I shot you— 'Bam'—right in the fucking head. That's a great story—straight

HBO." She leaned toward Terrance placing the gun lightly against his head. "How does that sound bitch?"

"I'm sorry." Terrance said, "You're right, I'm sorry."

She slid the gun down his cheek, the long muzzle caressing his pockmarked flesh. "Open up little bug," she said. "Open up, I want you to suck on this." She pushed the gun against his lips. Terrance kept his mouth firmly closed. "Open your fucking mouth," she demanded, "or I'll shove it in, and break your fucking teeth." Terrance reluctantly opened. She pushed the barrel between his thin lips.

"Now be a good little bug and suck it." Terrance sucked on the gun—the metal cold, leaving an acrid taste in his mouth.

"That's right," she cooed. "That's my little girl." Terrance sucked. "But don't suck too hard." She laughed, "You wouldn't want to make her cum."

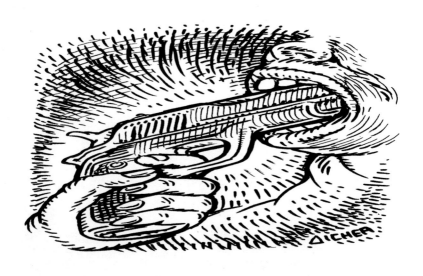

Terrance did as he was told. He dutifully sucked on the barrel—but as she said, not too hard. "That a girl," she said. "Look at you go."

"Gina!" A woman's voice yelled from the hilltop. "Gina!"

She jerked the gun out of Terrance's mouth—chipping a tooth and cutting his lip on exit. "Fuck!" Terrance cried. She wiped the wet barrel on the sleeve of her sweatshirt.

"I gotta go," she said. "Get it done little bug, or next time..." She waved the pistol at him, "...she's gonna cum. Now get the fuck out of here!" She slapped the side of his car and jogged up the hill. Terrance finally drove off.

****

He woke early. Normally Terrance rose at 4pm, had a quick breakfast of grapefruit and wheat toast—lightly buttered—*real butter, not spread,* before he headed over to Hedge's by 6, but not today. His sleep had been uneasy—fitful really. He'd been up and down all-night, and not just to urinate, something that he did on the average of three times an evening. He was troubled and he was having dreams of that awful woman. In the last, he was kneeling before her, naked, his ass exposed to the world, and he was sucking on her finger, licking ants off the tip—nasty little red ants that marched off her hand and drunkenly paraded down his throat. He could feel them sloshing about in his stomach screaming and vainly searching for a way out. He

163

shook his head to clear his thoughts, and then he grabbed his car keys and took the Fiesta for a drive. *"It really isn't such a bad car."*

He was a simple man who liked fires and, other than the illegalities associated with his trade, he was a law abiding citizen; paid his taxes, followed basic traffic rules and wasn't one to imbibe of spirits. Terrance took a wide turn on to Grand Avenue and headed downtown.

"Fires were pure and they were freeing," he thought. *"Not like being a policewoman, caging and harassing—I let things loose, let flames dance, I'm a creator and a watcher, and she is just... what the fuck?"*

Terrance had just driven past the large, indoor swap meet and got a glimpse of someone he thought he knew. He swung the car about, turned right on 16th and then parked at the 7-11 on Lincoln, before he walked back. He stood on the outskirts of the parking lot and stared toward the entrance of the stores. He was right; it *was* someone he knew; it was that crazy cop, and she was dressed in dark blue polyester. She sat in a chair, which seemed quite suited to her, right near the door, and she was armed.

"The bitch isn't a cop at all," Terrance thought. *"She's a guard, an armed security guard for a Mexican swap meet. How did she know about me? How did she find me? Wait, wait, maybe she's*

164

off duty, moonlighting, but no, no. Look at her, she belongs there, that's her chair—she is a guard—fuckin' A."

Terrance was furious, not only had he been scared near to death, but she'd made him suck that gun, and who knew where it'd been. *"And she's armed, the bitch is armed; she's crazy and they let her have a gun—what is this world coming to?"*

Just then, a man who looked to be of some importance, walked from the shops and confronted Terrence's nemesis, the man was yelling, and she was taking it, her shoulders slumped, her face sad, apologetic. Terrance was ecstatic. *"She must have fucked up at work and now she's getting reamed. Ha! I hope he cans that cunt! Fire her! Fire the bitch!"*

The man yelled a bit and then walked back the way he came— looking over his shoulder to make sure she was following, and then they both disappeared through the market's doors—her, puppy-dogging his heels as he led.

"Ain't so bold now—Miss, grab-my-crotch. I hope he's giving you what you gave me. Maybe she's sucking his 'gun' right now, ha! That'd teach her!" It was twenty minutes before Terrance saw her again. He had been gleefully watching the front door, fantasizing about her being punished and he almost missed her. She'd stormed from the back of the building—she was pissed— and Terrance rightly assumed that she'd been fired.

"I wonder what she did?" He mused. *"Probably got caught bullying customers or gun diddling. I sure hope he took the pistol."*

Terrance pulled the collar of his jacket up and acted painfully nonchalant as he watched her drop her keys twice while attempting to enter her car. When finally seated, she pounded the steering wheel in anger. Terrance was giggling. She started her vehicle, threw it into reverse and plowed into a shopping cart that tumbled over and got stuck beneath her bumper. This drew an all out guffaw from Terrence who then took the opportunity to run back to the 7-11 and grab his trusty Fiesta. He pulled around just in time to see her turn into traffic and drive off—her bumper noticeably scuffed. Terrance stayed a few car lengths behind. He was good at being nondescript, invisible—his whole life he had melted into the woodwork—at least until he had popped up on her radar. She drove toward the park on 7th and then turned into a rather run-down neighborhood near the channel. She pulled up to an old apartment building and parked, walked up a flight of stairs and unlocked the door to one of the units.

"This is more like it," Terrance thought. *"This is a place where a security guard might live, not a big 'ole house in the hills. I wonder how she ended up there anyway, wrapped up with that girl, sneaking around all night. I wouldn't be surprised if she bullied her too."*

166

Terrance checked his watch—not as nice as her timepiece—or as masculine, but it did the job. She was inside for a full hour before she walked down the stairs and got into her car. He was about to follow and pull in behind her, but she did a quick U-turn and headed back in his direction. He lay down in the front seat with his eyes closed—scrunched tight—and held still. He didn't breathe for the first fifteen seconds, but then he quickly exhaled, gasped, and held again. He waited for a pounding on the door, or even a broken glass entry demanding an explanation for his presence, but there was none. She hadn't seen him, and after a generous while he sat up to a clear coast. She was gone, and there was no way to know where.

Terrance decided to do some quick, safe recon. He walked up to the building, climbed the old concrete and metal staircase, got just high enough to see the number six on the door, and then retreated; stopping for only a second to check the mailbox—number six, G. Hernandez.

"Gina Hernandez," he said the name with contempt. *"It has to be her—a fucking security guard who lives in a shithole and pretends to be a cop."*

Terrance had heard of this sort of thing, he'd even seen a few of them on the freeway—men dressed as policeman, riding police bikes, pretending to be officers. *"I think it's a gay thing,"* Terrance thought to himself. He remembered seeing a movie somewhere of policemen having sex with each other. Terrance was frightened by the roughness.

167

"That would explain it, although I didn't know the girls did it too; and yet, there's the question of how she found me. I'm surely not gay."

Terrance wondered if he'd ever been near one of those rough clubs or in any way might have been close to... *"Wait, wait, wait, oh my God, I remember the car, her car, the blue Crown Vic. It was parked by the sporting goods store on 75th the night I torched it. I remember it now. I thought it was a couple of kids getting loose, having sex, making out, but it must have been her doing weird, cop-type things, sleazing about in the dark—fuck, she must have seen me, followed me—that sneaky whore, that nasty churro-guarding cunt."*

Terrence hurried back to his Fiesta, his ire rising. *"Oh, she'll pay for this alright. I'm not sure how, but she's gonna pay."*

He boldly ran his hand over his cut lip; his tongue did the same for his broken tooth. He'd get his revenge, but if he didn't get to work, he was going to be fired.

****

That night he did nothing—no watching, no burning, nothing, he just sat patiently and waited for her to arrive. At 4:45 a.m. her blue sedan skidded into the parking lot and as Terrance figured, she jumped out hot.

"What the hell are you doing?" she yelled. "Why the fuck isn't that house on fire?"

168

"I'm sorry," Terrance lied. "I had no way to reach you. I needed help. I knocked over a box inside and I couldn't pick it up. I couldn't just leave it, they'd catch me and I'd lose my job. Please, I couldn't leave it. I need help please!"

"You fucking little worm," the bull shitter now known as Gina said. "I told you I needed it done. I'll bust your fucking…"

"No, I swear I'll do it," Terrance pleaded. "I want to do it, just help me, there's still time if you help."

"Alright," Gina gave in. "What the fuck is it? What did you drop?"

"It's a box," Terrance said, "a big box and I couldn't lift it myself."

Terrance led the way into the storage units. The hallway was dark but as he cranked the timer switch the overhead fluorescents sputtered to life. "Hurry, hurry," he said. "It's not too big, but I can't do it myself. I need help."

She followed him down the corridors, Terrance turning switches as he walked from hallway to hallway—it was a tight maze of wooden doors and Master locks.

"Wait." Terrance stopped in front of a door marked Men's and shyly motioned to his crotch. "I gotta pee, OK?"

"Are you fucking kidding me?" Gina asked. "You gotta go tinky? Fucking pathetic little bug. Hurry the fuck up!"

Terrance entered the bathroom and shut the door. His stomach fluttering, he was as nervous as he'd ever been.

"*Fuck her,*" he thought. "*She made me suck that gun, she's going to hurt me—this is her fault, not mine, she's the liar.*"

He reached under the sink and grabbed a plastic bottle of Clorox and poured two fingers worth into an open tomato can that had been reserved for bathroom odds and ends—loose screws, knobs, etc. Terrance giggled because the pouring bleach sounded like a deep masculine whizz.

"What the fuck are you doing in there?" Gina demanded.

"I'm sorry." Terrance lied, "I just peed on my shirt."

"Oh, for fucks sake," Gina said. "Come on"

Terrance washed his hands and then for good measure, and extra protection, he grabbed the white, long-handled, toilet brush that was stored in a bucket by the john, and he opened the door. "Come on," Gina said, "what took so…" Terrance threw the bleach into her eyes. He dropped the can and jumped toward her, swinging the plastic brush. He connected a handle-bending blow to her head.

"Arrrrggggghhhh!" She screamed, clawing at her face, backing away from the blow. "My eyes, my fucking eyes!"

Terrance didn't let up; he swung again, the brush breaking over her arm—the plastic scrubbing head flying off, bouncing viciously and skidding down the hallway.

"What are you... Owww!" Terrance stabbed her with the broken handle; the cheap dirty plastic digging into her chest.

"I'll kill you, you little fuck! I'll kill you!" Gina became crazed, an injured animal, fighting for her life. She swung blindly, advancing toward Terrance—who, by the way, had not envisioned things progressing like this. She took a wide swipe and tore his face with her nails. Terrance turned terrified and ran—three hallways he traveled before he realized he was not being followed.

"Shit, shit, shit, shit," he said. "This is bad, this is real bad." He touched his face and flinched, pulling back fingers wet with clear ooze and blood. "Oh, fuck, listen to her!"

Gina was pounding and screaming—a blind bull thrashing against the walls.

"I have to stop it," Terrance thought. "Fuck. I have to stop this. What am I gonna do? Oh, God, what am I gonna do?"

Terrance checked his watch. He had time, but not much, something had to be done, he needed to be calm, he needed a second to think—to watch.

"OK, OK, she has to be stopped. I need something harder, something that'll knock her out."

Terrance ran toward the parking lot. He fished his keys out of his pants and opened the trunk of his car. He wildly fumbled about—not the least bit calm—and then he came up with a tire iron; a heavy, dirty, and slightly rusty, weapon of sorts. It would have to do. He ran back toward the building, threw open the door and Gina was there. She'd miraculously made her way to the exit—her eyes swollen shut—grabbing at Terrance. Terrance swung without thinking, a vicious tire-iron chop that landed brutally on her forehead. Gina's hands dropped immediately to her sides. She rag-dolled to the floor—blood instantly pouring over her face and onto the concrete.

"Fuck." Terrance stood, breathing hard, slightly shaking; watching her bleed. He kicked her with his foot, no movement. He kicked again, still nothing—her eyes still swollen and closed. He wasn't sure if she was dead, but she might be, it didn't look like she was breathing. Terrance took off his jacket and laid it over her face, covering her, and then he swung—a strong downward slash with the tire-iron. Then another, and another— four solid swings, each one undefended and well aimed.

Terrance stopped and dropped his weapon. It bounced off the concrete, clattered and lay still. She had to be dead; and now, he had to work quickly. Terrance tucked the edges of the bloody jacket around her head—wrapping her like a broken, bloody present, and then dashed off to find some better materials for the job. The day man would be here soon and this place was a mess. He had to tidy her up then square it away.

"Thank God I don't need help with that box," Terrance snickered.

There was a supply counter up front, not well stocked, this wasn't U-Haul after all, but there were some packing materials—tape, blanket pads, and bubble wrap. Terrance jumped the counter, grabbed a package of bubble wrap and a spool of "this is a real bitch to get off the roll," clear plastic tape—it would have to do.

There was quite a lot of blood and Terrance was glad he'd wrapped her head. He didn't want to look at her, and now, with her face covered, it was just arms, legs and a trunk—not human at all. He tore the bubble wrap out of the package, lifted her head and slid the plastic underneath. He then rolled her on to her side and pulled a full sheet about her before he wound the tape around. It wasn't hard, and the occasional popping bubble made it almost amusing. He struggled with the clear tape. Having no scissors or knife he attempted to tear it, but it was impossible, so he just kept wrapping until the roll was spent.

"Jesus, I need her car." He patted down her pockets and found the keys. There was a purple rabbit's foot attached to the ring, and a hard plastic picture of some fat kid. the young boy didn't look like her, at least as far as Terrence could remember, so it probably wasn't her kid, but who knows, Gina and the rabbit had now both been surgically altered.

Terrance hustled outside, jumped in her car and backed it up to the door. Her car stunk, wild-mountain pine-berry or some car freshener scent, it was thick, sickeningly thick.

"*Ha!*" Terrance thought. "*It would be weeks before they smelled a body in here, if that was the plan...*" But it wasn't, it was just nice to know that if Terrance got lazy—which he didn't—he could leave that crazy bitch in here and they wouldn't smell her for weeks. He smiled, relaxed, things were heading back to normal. He pulled the trunk latch and checked his watch again,

he had a solid forty-five minutes before Tony, the day man arrived—that is, if he showed up on time, he was supposed to be here at least fifteen minutes before clock-in and he was always late.

Terrance hopped out of the car and darted back into Hedge's. He grabbed Gina by her feet and dragged her outside. She was heavy, but the occasionally popping bubble wrap helped her slide. He dragged her over to the back of the car lifted the trunk lid and... "*What the fuck!*" Terrance recoiled in horror. There she was, the young blonde, eyes wide open and staring blankly at Terrance—dead as could be.

"*Oh, you nasty bitch.*" Terrance said, looking down at the bubble wrapped body. "*You nasty, nasty, bitch. What have you done? You killed her?*"

This wasn't going to be pleasant. He couldn't have that thing in the trunk starring at him as he loaded Gina in, it just wouldn't do. He ran back inside and grabbed a packing blanket from the store. *"Fuck, $10.99 for the blanket, $6 for the bubble wrap, and $2 for the tape, this is getting ridiculous."*

He went back outside, pulled the blanket out of the pack, shook it twice, then held it in front of him and advanced blind on the trunk. He covered the young girl's body and then tucked the blanket around it. She wasn't a big girl, but it wasn't a big trunk, and it was going to be tight. Terrance had to get Gina in now. He pulled her over to a sitting position against the car and then he kind of stood her up, her back to the trunk. It was a bitch—she was dead weight. He giggled, and had to slide her up and then push her back inside. The legs were easier. He lifted those up and just kind of folded her on top of herself. And then he stuffed her down and shut the lid. Terrance drove the car around the corner and parked it. It was too late to do what he needed to do and the car would be fine here. There was still blood on Hedge's floor and he needed to do a twice-over before he clocked out.

****

The next night Terrance arrived early to work refreshed and ready to go. He'd slept well—a bit disappointed at first, but well. The thought of him torching that home, watching that young girl flame-dance through the window had been exciting, and now it'd come to this. He grabbed a large plastic gas can from his car—he loved gas, easy to come by, getting a touch expensive, but so much fun to work with, quick, easy and a smell that could bring even a drunken man back from a stupor. He walked around the corner. Her car was as he left it: legally parked, fully registered, and fresh as a pine-mountain daisy. He opened the trunk and poured gas over the bodies—the air-freshener was overpowering. He shut the lid, unlocked the driver's door, put the keys in the ignition and liberally doused the interior before he locked up, leaving the plastic container inside; they were cheap, and untraceable, as if there would be anything left to trace.

"This is a joke," Terrance thought, *"a simple car job; a job for kids really. I should leave a yo-yo on the curb, but the police wouldn't get it. They're not as smart as her."*

Terrance pulled a lighter from his pocket and lit the end of a smoke—a nasty habit that he'd recently picked up—and thought about quitting, but the idea of never entertaining that cheery red smoke tip again was too sad to bear, so he took a long, thoughtful drag and gave up giving up.

He pulled a waxy piece of thick twine from his pocket, lit the end and tossed it into the pool of gas he'd spilt beneath the car. It ignited and the Crown Victoria was quickly consumed. Terrance turned his back and walked away. Cars never blew as fast as you see in the movies—it takes time, time and an experienced flame to get the right effect.

Terrance smiled, *"Yeah, this was a shit job, but there's a ripe house, Three-Thirty-Six, Sand Canyon Drive, waiting to burn. There is no sense in not fulfilling my promise to her. Of course it's no longer occupied, so my ménage à trois will have to wait, but that neighborhood, a canvas fitting for a master, well, that indeed, will be something to burn."*

The Evening Trees

The forest was a thousand lives old and the canopy of black sky that covered its boughs was held in place by a billion glittering stars. The Old Man stood on the edge of the wood gazing into the trees.

"Is there no way through?" He asked.

And this question was directed to no one in particular, because he stood alone, and as far as his eyes could see the forest ran a razor-sharp line through the world.

"How did I get here?" He wondered, "I was home in my bed—my nightclothes are proof of that, and yet here I am, and without pain."

He ran his hands across his 80-year-old frame, feeling his arms and chest. The dull, relentless ache that had plagued his days was gone, and he wasn't tired anymore. He wanted to tell his children that he was better, on the mend, wanting to walk the beach again, but they weren't there. No one was there, but him, and a forest that appeared impenetrable. He reached out and slightly touched the trunk of one of the trees. Its bark, if you could call it that, was smooth as human flesh stretched over bone—scarred and tanned to a deep winter brown. There was also something familiar there, a wave of memory that tried to come upon him, and would have washed over him, if his hand had stayed. He tentatively reached out again. A solitary wolf howled in the distance, but this time he held his palm firmly against the tree's flesh, and braced himself for the onslaught...

...Their shouts were in sharp contrast to the soft, blue, blanket he was wrapped in. He was a newborn, held in her arms and, at times, without thinking she squeezed him harder than she should have. She was screaming—her words in knife-tumbling flight at the target of her anger... a vanquished military man. "You're a loser," she screamed, "you don't care about our baby, about me, about anything. I fucking hate you, and I hate this," She recklessly held the child aloft. "You're a cheat, and a liar, and I wish he'd never been born."

The Old Man removed his hand from the tree. In the memory, he'd been that child, a tug-of-war witness to an argument between his parents; he was the fruit of his father's wandering lust and his mother's demented anger; and he hadn't been wanted.

As far as he could remember there'd been hostility in his childhood home, and why his parents stayed together, he never knew. He'd never seen them show affection to each other, or any kind of love. He had walked in on them having sex once— the military man ship-shaped and squared away on top of a submissively acting woman—her moans and faked "no" protestations giving cadence to his thrusts, but it wasn't love. In fact, to the Old Man's six-year-old eyes, it was ugly and violent.

It was strange, thinking of them now, in this foreign place, he hadn't thought of his parents in years—and he never remembered them looking as they did—his mother, even in her fury, so young and beautiful, and his father, so handsome in his uniform. When was the last time he'd seen them? His father had died of a heart attack when he was still a boy, and his mother had been gone some thirty years now. The last time he visited her she hadn't recognized him, and she was angry at his inability to stop the winter snow from filling her bedroom.

The Old Man sat on the ground, not frustrated, but unsure of how to proceed. It was then that she walked from the forest. He recognized her instantly, although her face changed with each step she took—she was his first wife, and then his youngest daughter, his last love, and then his eldest. She shimmered and shifted across the grass, until she stood before him, a masque of all the women he had ever loved.

"It's good to see you again." She said, her kind tones comforting him, reassuring. "You look well—older though, yes?" She smiled, the smile of his broken heart, but he felt safe and whole by her side.

"I'm not sure where I am," he said, "or what to do. Do you know?"

The woman lowered herself to the ground and reclined on the grass next to him. She wore a gown of sheer white, the naked lines of her body visible beneath the cloth, her light brown hair falling in long, soft, curls toward the ground. He waited until she spoke.

"You never get tired of looking to me for answers, do you?"

She was right; he'd always trusted the counsel of women, more so than he had men. He was surrounded by benevolent feminine angels—his business manager, his editor, and his best friend, all women. He was attracted by their strength and their kindness; although, when it came to lovers he usually fell for the domineering, unstable, unfaithful type—the opposite of what he craved.

"I think you need to walk through." She gestured toward the trees and, where there had been no path; there was now an entrance into the woods. "I think you need to go there; you love walking, and you'll find nothing in that forest that hasn't already hurt you."

She touched his forehead and brushed the ghost of his hair from his eyes.

"Do you know where I am?" he asked her. "Do you know why I thought of my parents?"

"Yes." She replied. "You're in bed, at home. Some of us are by you. Your daughters, Ana and Georgia, walked down to the cove; they're getting to know each other again. Your friend Julia is on the phone to your agent, and your manager is in the garden, crying, and talking to the press—you really had been quite the naughty boy, hadn't you?" She ran the back of her hand across his cheek and then lightly caressed his lips.

"And my mother and my father," he asked, "Why?"

"I think you just need to see." She said.

"Am I dead?"

"No," she replied, "not yet, but soon we hope."

The Old Man started to cry and she let him. There were times that he'd wanted to die—a few half-hearted suicide attempts, more out of frustration than sincerity—but in his later years he'd come to appreciate life, and now he selfishly clung to it, even as his body craved for release, he willed his soul to hang on.

"Come," she lovingly commanded the Old Man.

She helped him get to his feet and pulled him up into her arms. "I love you," she said, "and I was always so sorry that you couldn't feel it."

She walked with him toward the entrance to the woods, guiding his steps, and he followed like a child. He was a big man, a man who in his younger years intimidated and bullied other men, but he had always felt smaller when a woman was involved. He walked right to the edge of the forest and waited to follow her in.

"I'm not going with you," she told him. "This time, you go alone."

"Why?" he asked.

"Because you need to see what was hidden—what you refused to see in life."

He walked into the cool evening shade—the trees closed about him.

****

The woods were dark, but not unpleasant; they reminded him of a theatre, an empty house with the lights down, the trees were seats occupied by the unseen memories of his life, and he walked slowly down the cool, wooded aisle.

The Old Man was expecting his touch to release the past, but as he walked, he ran his hands along the trees and received no old thoughts to disturb him, and then ahead, the forest began to glow—a gentle light filling the space between a circle of trees. He heard the sounds of a playground—school-age children yelling with delight, laughing and extoling the glee of their days. Suddenly, the laughter turned vicious...

"It's a fight!" They yelled. "A fight!" The children were chanting, cheering on a recess battle with wild grade school yells. He moved closer. And now he was upon them, and among them. The children were standing in a circle blocking his view, the crowd jostling back and forth, side to side, surrounding the disturbance. They paid him no notice as he pushed his way forward; stepping into the group, trying to see what he knew he must see. Instantly, he was transported into the scene, cut and scraped by falling hard on the grade school blacktop...

... He'd been pushed down by a bigger boy—a lunchtime bully teasing him for his too large hand-me-down pants and shirt. He tried to get to his feet but he was brutally kicked between the legs, he went down again, and in an effort to distance themselves from the violence, his Cheerios and nonfat breakfast milk escaped from his stomach—the milk, as it hit the pavement, retaining its watered-down bluish tint. The children were cheering on his attacker, but from his vantage point on the ground he saw nothing but shoes—P.F. Flyers, All Stars, and Wallabees—dancing and stepping to the beat of the bully's blows.

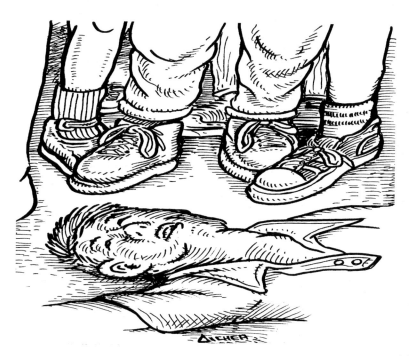

His cries were met with jeers and screams. No one came forward but the blows, and they, unmercifully falling... "Help me!" He screamed. "Please!"

He heard a woman's voice over the yells—familiar, pushing her way through the throng. "Let me through," she ordered, "let me through."

The children parted and from his place on the ground, he saw her shoes—his mother's cheap JC Penny pumps—and for a moment he thought he was saved as the bully's blows ceased. He raised his head toward her, the woman who gave him birth, but before his eyes could meet hers they traveled the lines of her face and nothing in that journey said comfort—she had the same contorted angry cheering lines that the children's faces held— and noting her fury, he knew there would be no sanctuary. His mother joined the chants. "Hit him!" she cried. "Hit him back!"

The children who at first were held at bay by the grown-up presence now renewed their anger, and the bully reared his fist back and fired a connecting no-help shot to his mouth. He was knocked cold.

When he awoke he was sitting with his back against a tree. The children were gone. He could hear his mother's pumps furiously marching off through the forest, but as his head cleared, it grew quiet. He touched his face, expecting dried blood and missing teeth, but he was whole. He was as unencumbered with physical pain, as he was when he began, but his heart was heavy. He remembered that day, and that beating, and the look on his mother's face as she refused his pleas. She thought she was helping him—encouraging him to be strong. She was wrong. He was a gentle child and wished no harm on others. He had counted on her to save him, to come to his aid, love, and protect him but, as always, he would be disappointed.

That was the last time he was ever beaten by another boy. He grew strong and the words, "*hit him*", had grown inside until her anger had blossomed like vicious flowers across his knuckles. Throughout his life, he had left a trail of beaten boys and men, all unknowing victims of his mother's twisted love. Strangely, he had never really wanted to hurt the men he fought. He felt sorry for them as they quailed beneath his blows. Somewhere under the hate instilled was that gentle boy cowering in a soft corner of his soul—that isn't to say that he wasn't vicious, because he had been. He'd been called a monster, a sociopath, soulless, and maybe at times he was—but his actions were an offering to the cruel Goddess he'd adored.

The Old Man stood and headed in the direction of his mother's echoing footsteps. He had no idea if the way was true, but the forest made itself hospitable to his path. As he walked, his thoughts drifted to his second wife—a woman cold of heart and withdrawn from his love. She was so much like his mother; not in looks, her blonde hair and light blue eyes were in sharp contrast to his mother's brown on brown, but in the way she loved, or rather withheld her love. There was a wall of distance around her that he could never breach no matter how hard he tried. Many days he acted as a willful child would, for it seemed that in her anger toward him, a slight connection was made, but she soon grew tired of his games and she withdrew further.

She'd been verbally accosted that day. Two twenty-something punks had thrown bargain-bin comments toward her ass as she walked past them into a shop. He was waiting for her in the car—she was to be quick, only a few items. He witnessed their exchange and did nothing. When his wife returned, she berated him for his unwillingness to act.

"What's the matter with you?" she demanded. "Didn't you hear what they said?"

"I thought it would be best to let it go." He was confused. She knew that he'd been working with a counselor—trying to reach the bottom of his rage. She shouldn't encourage this.

"You're a fucking coward, and you don't defend me."

She turned her back to him as they drove through the parking lot. He could picture her cold gaze freezing the windows of cars as they passed. He turned out and pulled up to a red light.

"That's them," she said, pointing at the two black-haired punks who were now casually driving away. He looked across her and saw them. They were in the right turn lane, oblivious—in an unsuspecting red Volkswagen getting ready to pull onto the

188

highway. His mother was now in the passenger seat of his car, although she was clothed in the bleached blond hair and plastic-titted body of his wife.

"You're a coward," she said. The cold indifference in her voice triggered something inside him. He yanked the wheel hard to the right, cut across traffic, and blocked the Volkswagen from moving. He was out of the car before she could protest—or encourage. The driver's window was down and before the driver knew what was coming; his head was slammed back into the headrest with a see-what-I-am punch to the face. It was immediately followed by a series of vicious blows delivered cold, but in hot procession one after another. The driver went unconscious, bleeding. People in the surrounding cars were honking now and he could hear screaming, muffled, coming over his shoulder. It was not unlike the children's voices from the playground, although these screams were not egging him on.

"Police!" Someone yelled. "Call the police!"

He slowed down and dimly became aware of what he was doing. The incident became a violent black marmalade dream that slowed his motion, dragging his actions to a stand still. The driver was barely lucid, moaning in his seat—the other boy, running terrified down the block. He walked back to his car and got in. The image of his mother was gone. His passenger was once again his wife, and his defense of her honor had softened her none. They divorced shortly thereafter.

He walked on.

The ground was soft beneath his feet, stepping over branch and fallen leaf. He inhaled and was comforted by the strong scent of pine and decaying brush—it would have been a pleasant walk but for the memories. And yet, he now had a slight sense of comfort knowing where his violence stemmed from. He'd done years of therapy, the counselors word-dancing around the influence of his mother, but he had never seen it as clearly as he did this day. The old schoolyard memory had lain silent until now, and the connection between the two had somehow freed him—*you did this, because of this*. It was so elementary in its simplicity and yet the rage he'd carried from a grade school recess had traveled some seventy years through his life. He checked himself, ran through various scenarios in his head— incidences where he might seek a violent solution to the situation—and it was as if the pathway of aggression had disappeared from his mind, he could see only peaceful, loving resolution in his head.

There was a light growing before him, a midmorning yellow glow, and his feet were no longer sinking into dirt. He was shuffling across the stained yellowed linoleum of his youth. Cheap floor tiles were now spread along the path and he tentatively walked into the kitchen of his boyhood home.

"What are you doing?" It was his mother. She was dressed in a short blue nightgown and nothing else. Her hair was undone,

190

loose and uncontrolled—her eyes matched.

He was stunned—not yet firm in his footing and then, instantly, he recognized the memory. He was in 7th grade and should've been in class.

"Why aren't you in school?" his mother asked.

"What are you doing home?"

He supplied as much of an answer as he did some years ago... none.

"I said, WHAT ARE YOU DOING!" she was demanding—the anger flushing her skin.

"I didn't go," he replied. "I didn't feel like it."

"You didn't feel like it?" She sarcastically questioned. "Do you feel like this?" His mother gestured to herself—a, "Valley of the Dolls," wannabe. "Do you feel like making me hurt?" She punched herself in the face.

"No!" He screamed. "Mom! Don't!"

She hit herself again—harder this time—closed fist blows knocking the false lashes from her eyes. She started screaming wildly and flailing her arms. "Look at me!" she screamed.

"Look at what you're doing to me."

"I'm sorry!" He yelled, "I won't... I'll go to school! I promise!"

She moved possessed across the floor—a broken mother toy unwound. She hit herself again and then swept her arm across the cluttered kitchen counter sending dirty plates and glasses crashing to the floor. *"LOOK AT ME! YOU DO THIS TO ME!"*

She fell to the ground, her arm cut and bleeding; her eyes now still, but rolled back beneath the sky blue lids. She lay there

sobbing—nightgown clenched high above her waist, exposed, open. She began to moan.

"Mom? Please," he begged her. *"I'm sorry. I'm sorry."*

No response.

He walked over to her, bent down, and straightened the nightgown over her legs and then he gently touched her arm. "Mom?" he asked, as if she was still someone else.

"Are you okay?"

The only answer he received was a low sorrowful moan—the sound of an animal injured on the highway—a voice somewhere below human.

"Should I call Dad?"

Still no answer.

He grabbed the hard plastic phone off the wall and rotary dialed his father's work. He was surprised he remembered the number after all these years. The secretary who answered was not pleased as his father was low man at the company and wasn't to be taking calls. He was informed that it was his son— a home emergency. "What's going on?" His father asked.

There was no, "hello," no, "are you okay?"

It was strictly, "god-damn-my-fucked-up-kid," business.

"It's Mom, she's not okay."

"What happened?"

It was an order, not a question.

"Where is she?"

"She's on the floor crying. She won't get up. She hurt herself."

"What did you do to her?" His father immediately accused.

"I didn't go to school. I..."

"God damn it! What the fuck did you do to her?" His father was furious.

He hung up the phone before the question could come again, "What did *you,* do to *her?"*

When he turned back to his mother she was gone and the broken glass on the floor began to shine. The kitchen turned into a forest glade and the bright pieces of the memory became the dappled sunlight on fallen leaves, it was over.

His mother had been ill—depressed and untreated. And his father, in an attempt to gain control of the situation had blamed him—he was the easy out. "Fuck." He swore to no one but him himself. His first wife was unstable—wild and dangerous. She cut herself when she was upset, torn scissor flesh held up as a testament to how he hurt her—*if only he hadn't done this, if only he hadn't said that.* He catered to her illness, babied her, and at times made love to her as the fresh cuts on her arm still bled. She was his mother. Immediately he recognized himself as Oedipus and was sickened by the thought, but it was true.

In his teen years he'd battled his father, toe to toe in violent front-yard stand-offs, and the heart attack that claimed his father's life, he was blamed for the stress that he had lain on the man. He inadvertently had killed his father.

It was a long walk now. Deep into the night he followed the path and no new memories came. It was almost as if the forest wanted him to ponder what he'd learned—to slowly chew over the pain of the truth until it was brutally digested in his soul. He began to hurt again. Wolves of self-pity were howling in the distance, moving closer and closer.

"Why?" He wondered. "Why me? I was a child. I didn't deserve what I had. I just wanted her love—I wanted their love. Why?"

His body shook with tears and he was tired. He didn't want to continue. He didn't want to hurt anymore, he just wanted to rest, but he moved on. All of them, he thought, those lovers who stood in her stead—surrogate mothers just as sick as his own—a sad chorus line of, cold, unstable women, who, try as he might, he could not help, and they would never love or support him as he wished. He had searched his whole life for that perfect love but he would never find it, because the world he searched in wasn't populated by his dreams but by the reality of his pain. Yet he had been surrounded by kind, loving women who adored him. They hated the choices he'd made, the pain he'd put himself through as he unknowingly sought to heal his first love, his mother, by attempting to save those sick women he chose. His friends and his daughters watched him fail, and loved him all the more for his unwillingness to give up, to walk away, and to turn his back on those that he thought needed his love most.

He felt something brush against his hip. It was a wolf—a large grey walking beside him. He was not afraid.

"You're part of me," he addressed the beast. "I knew you when I heard your voice in the trees. You prey on the weak and yet your hunger is never satisfied."

The wolf watched his face as he talked.

"All my life you've followed me, waiting for the moment the poison she planted would make me succumb—and you were close. I felt your foul breath against my neck as I swung from that rope and only fate and a broken beam spared me from your teeth. This forest has stripped the sheep's wool from my eyes, and from my heart. I'm no meal to you now. I'm free."

The forest opened onto a beach. The wolf disappeared and the Old Man walked out onto the sand. There were bodies of men, women and children lying in a lifeless pile—thousands of bodies.

****

"He's awake," it was his youngest daughter's voice.

He was lying in his bed, his body racked with pain; heavy, hard to breathe, but he felt them around him—the angels who had loved him.

"Father," his eldest spoke now. "You can let go Dad. We're here. We love you." He felt her squeeze his hand.

"I'm so sorry," he whispered. "I'm sorry that I hurt you. I just wanted their love—I wanted *her* love. I tried to heal those who could not be healed, and if I put you aside, or gave them love that was rightfully yours, I'm sorry. Please forgive me, my dears. I have always loved you."

He closed his eyes and stepped onto the pile of bodies. He climbed. They were stacked upward, toward the stars— thousands of the dead—a flesh stairway to the gods. He grew lighter as he rose, until he grew so light that he stepped from his body and was lifted up into the night.

About the Author

Jack Grisham lives with his wife Robin and their four children in a haunted schoolhouse in Huntington Beach California. He is a Hypnotist and a storyteller, a surfer, and the front man for the band T.S.O.L.

Jack is also the author of 'An American Demon' and frequently lives up to its name—but thankfully, not too often.

Call me: 1-714-969-9835
Twitter: Jack @jackloydgrisham
Website: www.jackgrisham.com
Email: jack@jackgrisham.com

More about the Author and the Book

Jack Grisham is a visionary. A man out of time. Always ahead. Ahead of me my whole life. Ahead of most people forever. Jacks is a poet. A creator. A comic. A madman, and dare I say... A genius of life. Now he adds author to all that! Holy Shit!

~ Bob Forrest ~ Thelonious Monster

Untamed, is stories soaked in sweat, blood, nightmare and punch-drunk desperation."
~ Wyatt Doyle ~ Publisher/NewTexture.com

Jack Grisham is the spawn of a Southern California upbringing: beach culture and punk rock, the bland repetition of suburban life, the innocuous blonde surfer boy with a (very) dark side. His writing is schooled and fueled variously by, "True Detective," magazine, Raymond Pettibone's comics, Charles Bukowski, "Mad" magazine and obvious hours spent in front of the TV as a tot and later in Detention. It's like a literary version of a grainy 1970's porn loop that ends as a snuff film. You'll either read this book cover-to-cover, or run from it, screaming, There's no middle ground.

~ Pleasant Gehman ~ Hollywood Icon

Other Punk Hostage Press Titles

Fractured (2012) by Danny Baker

Better Than A Gun In A Knife Fight (2012)
by A. Razor

Drawn Blood (2012) by A. Razor

The Daughters of Bastards (2012) by Iris Berry

Tomorrow, Yvonne. Poetry & Prose For Suicidal Egotists
(2012) by Yvonne de la Vega

impress (2012) by C.V. Auchterlonie

miracles of the BloG (2012)
by Carolyn Srygley-Moore

8th & Agony (2012) by Rich Ferguson

Beaten Up Beaten Down (2012) by A. Razor

Small Catastrophes in a Big World (2012)
by A. Razor

Moth Wing Tea (2013) by Dennis Cruz